PRAISE FOR HAZEL HOLT'S
MRS. MALORY SERIES:

MRS. MALORY WONDERS WHY
"Sheila's tart narration and her ear for the prevarications and evasions of her neighbors make her sixth outing an enjoyably crisp affair."
—*Publishers Weekly*

"A preference for scones at teatime, a penchant for sensible clothes, and a knack for solving crimes are all part of Mrs. Sheila Malory's irresistible British character."   —*Yakima Herald Republic*

"Another tidy tidbit for fans of traditional British-village mysteries."   —*Library Journal*

MRS. MALORY: DETECTIVE IN RESIDENCE
"Interesting . . . enjoyable . . . if you haven't discovered Mrs. Malory, I highly recommend reading the rest of the series."   —*Mystery News*

MRS. MALORY'S SHORTEST JOURNEY
"Highly entertaining . . . diverting, unexpected twists."
—*Booklist*

MRS. MALORY AND THE FESTIVAL MURDER
"A charming slice of British village life."
—*Chicago Sun Times*

THE CRUELLEST MONTH
"A soothing, gentle treat . . . the literate, enjoyable Mrs. Sheila Malory is back."
—*Atlanta Journal Constitution*

MRS. MALORY INVESTIGATES
"A British whodunit that works a traditional mode to good effect . . . delightful."
—*Cleveland Plain Dealer*

•HAZEL HOLT•

MRS. MALORY
WONDERS WHY

A SIGNET BOOK

SIGNET
Published by the Penguin Group
Penguin Books USA Inc., 375 Hudson Street,
New York, New York 10014, U.S.A.
Penguin Books Ltd, 27 Wrights Lane,
London W8 5TZ, England
Penguin Books Australia Ltd, Ringwood,
Victoria, Australia
Penguin Books Canada Ltd, 10 Alcorn Avenue,
Toronto, Ontario, Canada M4V 3B2
Penguin Books (N.Z.) Ltd, 182–190 Wairau Road,
Auckland 10, New Zealand

Penguin Books Ltd, Registered Offices:
Harmondsworth, Middlesex, England

Published by Signet, an imprint of Dutton Signet,
a division of Penguin Books USA Inc.
Previously published in a Dutton edition.

First Signet Printing, November, 1996
10 9 8 7 6 5 4 3 2 1

PUBLISHER'S NOTE
This is a work of fiction. Names, characters, places, and incidents either
are the product of the author's imagination or are used fictitiously,
and any resemblance to actual persons, living or dead, events, or locales
is entirely coincidental.

For my son Tom

since it was a vain attempt to
match his prodigious literary output that
got me into this situation in the first place

"**P**rofessional people are getting dreadfully *lax* nowadays," Mrs. Dudley said, spreading honey onto a scone with a slightly tremulous hand. "Do you know, Dr. Masefield came to see me the other day wearing a *sports jacket!*"

I expressed suitable horror at the enormity of this sartorial lapse. Over the years I have found that it's generally easier to agree with Mrs. Dudley's pronouncements than to present any other point of view, which she would, in any case, totally ignore.

"When I was a girl," she went on, "Dr. Campbell—he was Scottish, but from a very good family, his mother was a cousin of the Earl of Dunbar, I believe—wore a frock coat. And, even after the war, Dr. Browning always wore a dark suit." She stopped talking to wipe honey off her fingers with a small, finely embroidered linen napkin, then added, "I asked Dr. Masefield if he was going fishing, but he appeared not to take my point."

Mrs. Dudley is perhaps the most difficult of what my son, Michael, calls my Coven of Old Ladies, but since she is the mother of my best friend, Rosemary, I try to visit her fairly often. And, as a middle-aged widow, I find it comforting in a way, to step back into the past and be with someone who remembers me as a child and still thinks of me as a young person. It's pleasant, too, in what has become for everyone these days a very busy and often stressful life, to go out to tea occasionally in the old-fashioned way. Tea with Mrs. Dudley is always a traditional occasion with bread and butter, scones (in the summer) or crumpets (in the winter), homemade jam, and at least three kinds of cake made by her elderly slave Elsie, whose Victoria sandwich is acknowledged to be the finest in the whole of Taviscombe.

"Dr. Masefield is not particularly satisfactory in other ways," Mrs. Dudley continued. "He completely failed at first to diagnose what was wrong with me when I had that terrible gastric trouble last year."

That trouble, as Rosemary told me with some asperity, was caused by Mrs. Dudley eating four scones, thickly spread with strawberry jam and clotted cream, followed by a large slice of coffee-and-walnut cake. Dr. Masefield's final diagnosis ("A touch of gastric flu—there's been a lot of it about just now") had been, given his knowledge of Mrs.

Dudley's intractable determination to ignore all advice she didn't wish to take, a masterpiece of diplomacy.

"You have Dr. Macdonald, of course," she went on. "I did go to him for a short time, but he was never what I would call satisfactory."

Mrs. Dudley had often explained that she was a private patient because, "I believe you get what you pay for in this life, and I do feel that one's health is too important to be left in the hands of the— What is it they call it?—the *National* Health Service." Thus, she tended to shop around, as it were, for her medical advisers. Fortunately Taviscombe, because it is a seaside town with a high proportion of geriatrics, has a great many doctors to the square mile. Mrs. Dudley has worked her way through most of them.

"All this newfangled nonsense he goes in for," she said scathingly. (Dr. Macdonald now has his patients' records on a computer.) "And all this going off on *courses*"—a wealth of scorn in the word— "instead of looking after his patients properly. I'm sure if your poor mother had had proper medical attention from some *reliable* doctor, she would have been with us today."

"Mother was perfectly happy with Dr. Macdonald, and so am I," I said.

"Not that his partner, Dr. Frobisher, is any better," Mrs. Dudley went on as if I had not spoken.

"*Drink,* of course. I've seen him several times coming out of the Kings Head."

"Perhaps he had been visiting a patient there," I suggested, more to keep the conversation going than with any expectation that Mrs. Dudley would accept my explanation.

"No doubt that is what he would have us believe," she said darkly. "But I know better."

Mrs. Dudley makes a practice of knowing better than anyone else.

"Of course, the *real* drinker was old Dr. Bright. You remember when he ran into another car that night at Sully Corner and was prosecuted for drunken driving!"

This incident formed part of the folklore of Taviscombe—much discussed even now by the older ladies of the town—and had happened when I was ten. Mrs. Dudley has this habit of treating me simultaneously as a child and as a contemporary, which is sometimes confusing.

"Then there was Dr. Phillips. Now that was *quite* a while ago, during the war—he left his wife and went off with a Land Girl. I was really shocked—he seemed a thoroughly nice man, very sympathetic when I was so dreadfully upset that time Rosemary had scarlet fever. It just shows," she concluded triumphantly as if summing up a judicial inquiry, "you can't really trust any of them."

She raised a silver serving knife ceremoniously above Elsie's cherry-and-walnut cake and cut a large wedge. My capacity for cake is not what it was in the days when, as a hungry schoolgirl, I used to go to tea with Rosemary, but I know my duty and I began to work my way through it as Mrs. Dudley continued her survey of the Taviscombe medical scene. She progressed relentlessly through the years up to the present day, finding in them all some fatal flaw.

"Dr. Morris never listens properly to what you say to him. I never cared for his manner; very abrupt. But he is, in any case, a rather common sort of man—it really is amazing the sort of people who are allowed into the medical profession these days! They're all young boys, and there is scarcely a doctor in Taviscombe now who could be described as a gentleman."

"There's Dr. Cowley," I suggested.

"Dr. Cowley!" Mrs. Dudley gave me a sharp look. "My dear Sheila, I wouldn't go to Dr. Cowley if he was the last doctor on earth! I grant you he's not young—I suppose he must be nearly seventy now and his manners are perfectly respectable, but . . . well . . . think of Mrs. Endicott, *and* Mrs. Faversham-Browne! Quite large sums of money they left him, I believe. You will never persuade me that he didn't hasten their ends, poor souls. And there was old Miss Benson—that was never properly cleared up. You wouldn't remember that—it was years ago. The nephew went to court, you know; claimed undue influence. Of course Dr. Cowley got away with it, that sort always does, but his practice has fallen off quite considerably since then! No, I find Dr. Cowley a very questionable sort of person."

Loath as I always am to agree with any pronouncement of Mrs. Dudley's, I do feel as she does about Dr. Cowley. He is, it must be admitted, a perfectly respectable man in late middle age, with a style that his elderly patients (and they are all elderly, the young finding him old-fashioned in his manner and his methods) seem charmed by. I have always found his turn of speech fulsome and somehow distasteful. "Smarmy," my friend Rosemary says in her usual robust way, and it does rather sum him up.

"I must say, I don't particularly care for him myself," I said, surreptitiously loosening the belt of my skirt to accommodate the cherry-and-walnut cake.

"And I believe he's after that house on West Hill," Mrs. Dudley said. "You know, where the Martins used to live."

Dr. Cowley was a great purchaser of property. In addition to his own handsome house in Park Walk, he also owns several houses in the town.

"I hadn't heard that," I said, intrigued—as always—by Mrs. Dudley's ability to be first with any piece of news or gossip. "But he already owns one house on West Hill—Kimberley Lodge—it's divided up into flats: Miss Graham lives in one of them."

"Exactly!" Mrs. Dudley said triumphantly. "The Martins' house backs up to that one. I had heard that he's thinking of putting the two together and making them into a nursing home. He could make a fortune!"

"Goodness!" I exclaimed. "Another nursing home!"

Taviscombe is rich in such places, but, I have to admit, there's always room for one more.

"But two of the flats are occupied," I protested, "and I don't imagine he could get possession very easily."

"Oh, poor little Miss Graham could go at *any* time," Mrs. Dudley said dismissively. "She's nearly ninety and she's had a weak heart for years—one bad go of this summer flu that's about just now would finish her off."

Miss Graham was only a few years older than Mrs. Dudley and, although a little frail, in perfect health. Mrs. Dudley, convinced of her own immortality, tended to view members of her own generation as inferior specimens liable to succumb to any passing ailment.

"Anyway," I said, reluctantly drawn into this speculation, as one always is with Mrs. Dudley, "there's Mrs. Wheatley in the other flat. She's only about my age, and I haven't heard that *she's* moving."

"Oh, I daresay he'll find some way of getting rid of her," Mrs. Dudley said airily. "Besides, she has a very *dubious* reputation, as you know." Mrs. Wheatley was reputed to be the mistress of a wealthy businessman from Bristol who was alleged

to have "set her up" in the flat she now occupied.
There was no actual evidence for this, other than
her appearance (obviously expensive, too smart for
Taviscombe clothes, and rather too much makeup—
worn even when shopping early in the day) and the
occasional visits she was seen to receive from an
elderly man, who might perfectly well have been a
relation. However, the fact that she didn't go to
church, shunned Taviscombe society in general, and
had refused (though perfectly politely) to take part
in the many bazaars, bring-and-buy sales, and coffee
mornings that formed the basis of Taviscombe life,
naturally made her an object of suspicion and speculation among Mrs. Dudley's circle of friends. Actually, she had always seemed to me a perfectly nice
woman. She greeted me civilly enough whenever I
happened to meet her going out of Kimberley
Lodge, when I was visiting Miss Graham. But I
knew that it would be useless to suggest such a
thing to Mrs. Dudley.

I said as much to Rosemary when I met her outside Woolworth the following day.

"Oh, Mother gets more impossible every day!" she
exclaimed. "Do you know, she's decided she *has* to
have a new outfit for the Conservative Ladies
lunch—I mean, she's got a wardrobe full of things
she's hardly ever worn! So I've got to go to Estelle's
to look for something suitable and then take a selection for her to try on, and she probably won't like
any of them so I'll have to take them all back again,

and Estelle will *look* at me, you know the way she does!"

Estelle, who ran Taviscombe's most exclusive dress shop, knew Mrs. Dudley of old and knew that she would, in the end, buy one or even two horrendously expensive garments. But her scornful manner was always extremely daunting to all but the strongest spirits, and I felt deeply sorry for Rosemary, caught between such a Scylla and Charybdis, her mother and Estelle.

"Oh, poor you!" I said sympathetically. "Her things are so expensive nowadays—I never go there except sometimes when she has a sale, and she despises sale customers so much that she usually leaves them all to that wretched downtrodden assistant, so one is safe from her contempt!"

"Mother could perfectly easily go herself. She's quite well now, but she's got into the way of having things brought to her—like royalty, you know—so she's not going to give that up in a hurry!"

"Is it true, though," I asked, reverting to the subject on my mind, "that Dr. Cowley's going to open a nursing home?"

"Well, Mother's usually right about things like that," Rosemary said, stepping out of the way of a shopping cart imperfectly controlled by an elderly woman whose progress was already impeded by a small and excitable dog. "It would make sense, I suppose, him being a doctor and so forth. And he's got just the sort of horrid ingratiating way about him that would go down well with the patients' relatives, I should think."

"Oh, dear," I said. "I do hope poor Miss Graham has a proper lease. I must ask Michael. I think it's his firm that acts for her. Actually, I must go and see her soon, poor soul. Her rheumatism has been quite bad, and she hasn't been able to get out much lately."

I made a batch of scones to take to Miss Graham. She's quite fit really and can look after herself perfectly well, but she is an absolutely terrible cook, always has been—she and my mother used to have little jokes about it—and, since she has a sweet tooth, she is very appreciative of any homemade goodies one may take.

"Oh, my dear Sheila," she said as she put the scones into a tin, "what a treat! I've got a nice pot of gooseberry jam that I got at last month's bring-and-buy sale at the church hall; they'll be lovely with that. Now do come and sit down and tell me all about what Michael is doing these days. Of course he's with Drayton and Decker now, isn't he? You must be so pleased he followed in dear Peter's footsteps."

"Yes, it's marvelous that that seems to be what he wants to do. I'm so lucky that he loves being here in Taviscombe; so many young people seem to want to live in London, or even abroad."

"Well," Miss Graham said, "Taviscombe has always been good enough for me."

"Me, too," I said, looking out the large window at the sea stretching far away to the horizon, with hills and promontories misty in the distance. "We're so lucky to live in such a beautiful place."

"That's what I was saying to Ronnie the other day," Miss Graham said. "He was talking about moving to Manchester, if you please. I said to him, 'You won't like it there, a big city like that!' "

Ronnie was Miss Graham's nephew, who owned the larger of the two shoe shops in Taviscombe.

"Why Manchester?" I asked.

"Oh, something about a shop there that might be a good business prospect. I'm afraid I didn't really understand what it was all about. But I do know he would miss the countryside and the birds—he's such a keen bird-watcher."

"Well," I said reasonably, "they do *have* countryside up there—it's not far from the Lake District, you know—and probably birds as well, and I daresay business would be better for him in a large city."

"Oh, no," Miss Graham answered, shaking her head dismissively. "He wouldn't like it at all! No, it's that wife of his. She'll never be satisfied until she gets him up north somewhere. I always said it was a mistake for him to marry a northerner."

Ronnie's wife, Carol, came from Staffordshire, but to Miss Graham anywhere beyond Bristol was irretrievably "northern" and, as such, suspect.

"He seems to be doing quite well in Taviscombe," I said. "I mean, there usually seem to be several customers in the shop whenever I go by. There's always a good selection of larger sizes, and Carol is very helpful about ordering things." I spoke with feeling, since I have what are known as "difficult" feet.

"Oh, well," Miss Graham said grudgingly. "I suppose she's quite useful in the shop and it does save him having to pay another assistant, but she's a terrible one for laying down the law. The poor boy can't call his life his own, either at home or in the business!"

I made little murmuring noises as if of agreement, but in my opinion it's only Carol's efficiency and determination that keep that particular business going. Although I'm sure he has a sweet nature—he's very kind to his aunt—Ronnie has always seemed a rather dreary man, colorless and ineffectual, who needs a good push from a stronger personality to achieve anything at all.

"So are they going?" I asked.

"Oh, nothing's settled," she replied. "I think she went up there to look at the property but I don't think they've made an offer yet."

"Well," I said, "I hope for your sake that they don't go. You'd miss Ronnie if he was that far away."

"Indeed I would. He's such a thoughtful boy. I know I can always call on him if I want any little job done; he put a plug on my new kettle the other day—it's so awkward getting anything like that done if you live alone. You can't get a man in to do it. I mean, they don't like coming out for a little thing like that."

Miss Graham got up from her chair.

"Talking of which," she said, "do let me get you a cup of coffee."

She trotted off into the kitchen, and I stood by the window, watching the seagulls wheeling and swerving in the blue summer sky. Below, the tide was out and tiny figures walked upon the beach or engaged in aquatic activities at the water's edge.

"This *is* a nice flat," I said, turning as Miss Graham came back into the room with a tray. "You're so lucky to have this lovely view."

"Oh, yes," she replied, handing me a cup of rather too milky coffee. "I really was so fortunate getting it like that. Of course Dr. Cowley has always been my doctor, so when this flat fell vacant he mentioned it to me at once, and of course I jumped at the chance! I always say I have the best of all possible worlds living here—that beautiful view of the sea and the hills, without any of the trouble those people who live on the quay so often get."

"Yes, I don't think I would want to live there," I agreed.

"Visitors staring into your windows, and *worse*," she added darkly. "Young people can be so *rowdy* nowadays. Drinking and goodness knows what! Mrs. Phillips—you know, she lives in that cottage right by the harbor—told me you wouldn't believe how some of them go on!"

"No," I said, "you're much better off up here. What's Dr. Cowley like as a landlord?"

"Oh, he's such a charming man!" Miss Graham answered and smiled, "so good about having things done. I have only to ask! And the gardens are very well kept. Fred Lipman—he's one of Dr. Cowley's patients—comes once a week to keep them in order. Yes, I'm very lucky."

I didn't have the heart to inquire if she'd heard anything about Dr. Cowley's plans for a nursing home, but when Michael came home that evening I asked him about Miss Graham's lease.

"I mean," I said, "if Dr. Cowley's up to something I'd hate to think that poor Miss Graham didn't have secure tenure, or whatever it's called."

"I'll look it up," he promised absently. "I say, Ma, can you possibly give me a lift to Taunton and back tomorrow? My car's got to go in for its M.O.T. and I'd forgotten I've simply got to go to the Land Registry. You could do some shopping while you waited for me," he suggested hopefully.

"You could go by bus," I said, knowing perfectly well that I would provide the chauffeuring service I had been providing, on and off, for the last twenty-three years.

Michael grinned. "Bless you," he said. "I'll do the washing up tonight in payment—oh, no, sorry, I can't. I've got to slip out after supper and see Jonah. Tell you what, I'll buy you a G and T at the County tomorrow instead."

*   *   *

I WAS SITTING in the Wyvern Bar of the County
Hotel in Taunton, waiting for Michael. I'd bought
myself an orange juice (since I was driving) and ham
roll because shopping always makes me hungry. The
roll was not so much a roll as a hunk of French
bread, almost impossible to eat gracefully, and I was
really quite glad that there was nobody I knew to
see me maneuvering it into my mouth. But, when
I'd eaten most of it and brushed the flaky crumbs
off the front of my blouse, I had time to look around
me, and I saw that there were indeed two people I
knew in the bar. Seated at a small table in the corner were Dr. Cowley and Mrs. Wheatley. Luckily
they were much too occupied with each other to
notice me.

· 2 ·

Somehow I didn't want them to know that I'd seen them—an atavistic feeling that secret knowledge is power over other people, or something like that—so I took out a copy of *The Spectator* that I'd just bought and opened it up. Peering over the top, I continued my observation of this unlikely couple. Well, not *totally* unlikely, I suppose. Dr. Cowley was Mrs. Wheatley's landlord, after all, and also her G.P., and they could perfectly well have met by chance, but somehow, watching them, I was convinced this was no casual meeting. They seemed very absorbed in each other, he bending deferentially toward her to catch her remarks—she had a very soft, rather shy voice—and she with her head bowed, apparently looking at some sort of document on the table before them. I strained forward to try to catch a glimpse of what it might be, but they were too far away for me to see. I toyed with the idea of getting up and walking past their table but reluctantly abandoned that because if I got that close to them, they would be certain to recognize me.

My thoughts were interrupted by Michael's voice saying, "What on earth are you doing, Ma, hiding behind that magazine like someone in an inferior thriller?"

I frowned at him and made flapping gestures for him to sit down and be quiet.

"Keep your voice down!" I whispered. "I want to see what's going on over there—no! *Don't* turn round."

Michael shook his head in mock sorrow.

"I don't know about you," he said. "You've finally flipped!"

"Don't be silly," I said sternly. "It's Dr. Cowley and Mrs. Wheatley. Over there—it's so very odd to see them together."

"This passion for gossip is most unbecoming, you know."

"It isn't gossip," I said impatiently. "Well, yes, in a way it is, but I really don't trust that man, and Mrs. Wheatley does live in the flat above Miss Graham, and there *are* all sorts of rumors about what he might be going to do with that property. And why are they meeting here in Taunton away from prying Taviscombe eyes?"

"Illicit love?" Michael suggested.

"Don't be ridiculous!" I replied. "Anyway, there's

no reason for it to be *illicit* on either side, as far as I know."

"I thought Dr. Cowley was married," Michael said.

"No, he's a widower. And she doesn't appear to have any ties—well, not if you discount the rumors about her 'protector.' I do wish I could see what they're studying so earnestly. Tell you what, they don't really know you by sight; go and get yourself a drink and a sandwich, and see if you can find out what they're looking at."

I waited impatiently for Michael to come back.

When he did, he carefully put down a half pint of bitter and a plate with two large rolls and two Danish. "I didn't get you another drink, but I thought you might like a Danish. Would you rather have the apple or the one with squishy bits of almond paste?"

"Whichever," I said. "It doesn't matter. Well? Did you see?"

Michael took a maddening pull at his beer before replying.

"Vile stuff," he said. "Can't think why I drink it."

"Michael!" I said and glared at him.

"Oh, yes, your chums. They were looking at holiday brochures."

"What!"

"Sh! They'll hear you if you go around bellowing like that. They were leaflets about cruises. Looks as if they're planning an elopement or something."

"But they hardly know each other!" I protested.

"Doesn't look like it from here," Michael replied.

"Well, no, I must say, they do seem pretty chummy. I wonder what they were saying. Did you hear anything?"

"He was just extolling the delights of Madeira."

Michael tipped one of the pastries onto my empty plate and started into a ham roll.

I saw Dr. Cowley take another sheet of paper from his briefcase and lay it on top of the brochures.

"Michael," I said, "I need a fork for this pastry. Would you go and get me one, please. Oh—and, on your way, see if you can see what that new sheet of paper is, the one they're looking at now."

"Oh, Ma, really!"

"Go *on*, before he puts it away again."

Michael got up reluctantly and made his way past their table once more. He came back with a fork and a paper napkin.

"Here, for your sticky fingers." He took a large bite out of the remaining roll.

"Well?" I asked impatiently.

"Looked like plans," Michael said briefly, his voice muffled by ham roll.

"Plans?"

"Building plans. And he was saying something about it being a splendid opportunity not to be missed."

"There!" I exclaimed. "He *is* going ahead with that nursing home scheme! Poor little Miss Graham!

25

And *what* is he up to with Mrs. Wheatley? She always seemed a perfectly rational woman. How *could* she allow herself to be taken in by that awful man!"

"Stop fulminating," Michael said, "and eat up your nice Danish. I've got to be getting back. I'm supposed to be completing another conveyancing this afternoon, and the clients will be jumping up and down if I'm late."

As we drove back, I reminded Michael of his promise to look up Miss Graham's lease.

"If it's a while ago, then I expect Edward drew it up himself," he said, "so it should be pretty watertight; you know how thorough he is."

"I still can't get over Dr. Cowley and Mrs. Wheatley," I said. "Even Mrs. Dudley didn't know about *that!*"

"Why shouldn't they get together?" Michael asked. "Two old birds going off for a holiday, what's wrong with that?"

"I'm positive he's trying to wheedle his way round her somehow," I said, steering cautiously past a heavily ladened tractor. "Either to get her out of her flat or—yes, of course—the plans and all that bit about it being an opportunity! He's trying to get her to invest in the thing!"

I tried this theory on Rosemary when she came round the next morning to collect some jumble for the Red Cross.

"Fancy! Those two!" Rosemary said. "Who'd have believed it!"

"I expect he's been worming his way into her confidence for ages," I said as I measured some coffee into the machine. My efforts were impeded by Foss, my Siamese cat, who considers the kitchen countertop his domain and feels bound to investigate any activity that takes place there. Fortunately Rosemary is at least as silly about animals as I am and doesn't in the least mind having a black-masked Siamese face poked inquiringly into the coffee she is about to drink.

"How far do you think it's gone?" Rosemary asked. "I mean, do you think he's prepared to marry her to get at her money?"

"Perhaps being married would cramp his style with the other middle-aged widows and elderly ladies," I suggested unkindly. "Biscuits with your coffee?"

"No, I daren't. I need to lose at *least* half a stone. I simply can't get into that flowered dress I bought last summer. You know, the blue-and-white one that opens down the front—it gapes quite hideously at *all* the buttonholes if I try to do it up over the stomach! I think I'll try that fiber diet. It sounds disgusting, but at least you get something filling to eat."

Rosemary is a dedicated beginner of diets. I've more or less given up, except when I suddenly see the reflection of a large-hipped woman in a shop window and realize with horror that it's me.

"Of course," I said, reverting to the subject uppermost in my mind, "there was some sort of mystery about his marriage, wasn't there? Something about his wife dying abroad?"

"I think it was Portugal," Rosemary said, picking up Foss and cradling him in her arms. "Who's a beautiful boy then?" she inquired lovingly. Foss gave a loud cry, presumably of agreement, and she went on, "Or was it Italy—yes, that's it, Rome. I remember thinking that she might be buried in the English cemetery there with Keats."

"What were they doing in Rome?" I asked. "On holiday or what?"

"No, I think he had some sort of job there for a while, and he came back to Taviscombe when she died. I must ask Mother. She'll know."

"Perhaps the wife isn't dead at all," I speculated. "Perhaps she's still there, living abroad somewhere. That would cramp his style with Mrs. Wheatley!"

"I shouldn't think a little thing like bigamy would stop him," Rosemary said airily. "Not if it stood in the way of his plans. I mean, nursing homes are absolute *gold mines* now, especially for the elderly, and especially here. I should think the average age of the population in Taviscombe nowadays is about seventy-five. Honestly, as I said to Jack the other day, it's ridiculous at our age to find ourselves the youngest people at practically every social gathering! No, if you can offer residential *and* nursing care, you can charge the earth. People are desperate!"

"It is depressing," I said. "I always pray that I'll

go quickly and not hang on for ages being a burden to my nearest and dearest and gobbling up all their inheritance with nursing home fees!"

"And him being a doctor, of course," Rosemary continued, "would be a terrific plus point with the relations. It would add *plausibility*!"

She finished her coffee and put Foss gently down onto the floor. "I must be going. I've got to change Mother's library book, and there's never anything in there she wants to read. We've been through the biography section pretty comprehensively, and she doesn't like novels because of the *language*—not that I blame her there—perhaps there'll be a Dick Francis she hasn't read."

Mrs. Dudley had this unexpected passion for racing, presumably because of the royal connection. "Oh, well, whatever I get, it'll be wrong . . ."

We went out into the hall to pick up the jumble. Rosemary opened one of the bags.

"What a splendid haul! You *have* been having a jolly good clear-out! Are you sure you want to get rid of this navy skirt—I always thought it really suited you."

I groaned.

"Too tight at the waist! I tried moving the button, but it hung all peculiar. Yes, I know, I *ought* to lose a couple of inches, but life's too short, especially when I have to cook all those hefty meals for Michael. I expect that's why I've put on these extra pounds since he's been back home. But if I do try just to toy with a lettuce leaf and a yogurt, he complains that it's antisocial. And anyway," I said defiantly, "I suppose I just like food! It's awful, really, that one should have to feel so defensive about it these days."

I opened the front door, and we stood looking out at the gray, overcast day, not helped by the low cloud hanging over the hills.

"Isn't it miserable?" Rosemary said. "I bet it rains for Wimbledon. I must say, on days like this, I wouldn't mind a glamorous foreign cruise."

"But *not*," I said, "with Dr. Cowley!"

A FEW DAYS LATER I was just rolling out the suet crust for a steak-and-kidney pudding (Michael's favorite food, even in the summer) when the phone rang. It really is amazing how often the phone rings at awkward times—hands covered with flour, hair dripping with shampoo, halfway through defleaing a recalcitrant dog—when there are vast tracts of time—long, gray winter afternoons, for example—when one *longs* for it to ring and it remains obstinately silent. Rather resentfully, then, I picked up the receiver. I must have sounded a bit abrupt because Miss Graham, at the other end of the line, immediately became very flustered.

"Oh, dear, have I rung at a difficult moment? I'm *so* sorry—I'll ring some other time, but I was rather worried . . ."

She trailed off into incoherence, and I pulled myself together.

"No! It's absolutely fine," I said. "Please, do let me know what's the matter."

"Well, dear, it's this *letter* I've had. I would have rung Ronnie about it, but Carol always makes a bit of a fuss if I ask him to do anything for me—just between ourselves, she's not really a very nice person—so I thought perhaps you would help me. You've always been so kind, just like poor Peter and your dear mother. It came right out of the blue. I was so taken aback—the last thing I expected! It really is very disturbing and I simply don't know *what* I should do for the best, so you do see I *would* appreciate your advice."

"Who is the letter from?" I asked, when at last she paused for breath.

"Oh, dear, didn't I say? You see what a state I'm in! It's from Dr. Cowley."

"I see," I said. "Look here, how would it be if I came round tomorrow—would about ten-thirty be all right?—and you can show me the letter and we'll see what it's all about."

"Oh, my dear, that would be kind! I'm sure you will be able to tell me what to do."

I hoped her confidence in me wouldn't be misplaced, and, after I'd put the steak-and-kidney pudding on to steam, I threw together a few fairy cakes to take with me, hoping they might exercise a calming influence. Miss Graham was still pretty upset when I arrived at the flat the next morning.

"I'm so glad you've come, Sheila. I hardly slept a wink last night worrying about it all. Here," she said as she thrust a letter into my hand. She sat down in the chair opposite me, fixing her eyes on me *trustingly,* rather as my little dog Tris does when his ball has rolled behind the sideboard and he wants me to get it out for him.

The letter from Dr. Cowley was not unfriendly in tone, but the contents were quite enough to agitate an old lady. He set out his proposals for turning Kimberley Lodge and the neighboring property into a nursing home and said that, although he realized that her lease had some years to run, he would be prepared to make a cash settlement and find her alternative accommodation if she would vacate her fiat within six weeks. He was sure that she would see the advisability of agreeing to this proposition, since he had long felt that the situation of Kimberley Lodge—on such a steep hill and a distance from the shops—made it unsuitable for her now that she was not as mobile as she had been. Altogether it was a thoroughly unpleasant letter, the ruthlessly self-interested motives imperfectly masked by a hypocritical concern for her welfare.

"Goodness," I said, "what a repulsive man he is!"

"He's always been so charming," Miss Graham said sadly, "such a gentlemanly man, I thought, but now this . . ."

"I've never liked him," I said, "and neither did Mother. We always felt that his manner was false somehow. Well, he's certainly shown himself in his true colors now! Obviously you don't want to move, whatever alternative accommodation he offers you."

Miss Graham's air of bewilderment was replaced by one of grim determination.

"This is my home," she said. "I don't want to go moving at my age. Besides, I've always wanted to live up here on West Hill, looking out over the sea, ever since I was a girl. It was a dream come true when Dr. Cowley offered me this flat. And I have got a lease. Surely he can't make me move."

"No, I'm sure he can't," I said soothingly. "Look, can I take the letter to show Michael? Since his firm drew up the lease for you, I'm sure they'll be able to advise you."

"Oh, would you, dear? That would be good of you. I'm so bad at explaining things, but I know you'll be able to make them understand that I simply couldn't bear the upheaval of moving somewhere else, not to mention leaving this flat. Now that I can't get out so easily, it means so much to me to have all this to look out at—apart from the lovely view, there's always something going on, something interesting. You do understand, don't you, Sheila? I'm not making a fuss about nothing, am I?"

"Certainly you're not," I replied warmly. "Of *course* it means a lot to you, and, as you say, it is your home. We'll sort something out, don't you worry. Now, shall I make us both a nice cup of tea? And do let me know what you think of these little fairy cakes."

THAT EVENING at supper, I showed Dr. Cowley's letter to Michael. "The miserable old sod!" Michael said, and although I deplored his language, I certainly agreed with the sentiment.

"Well, now," he continued, "I don't think that legally he has a leg to stand on. Of course we'll have to have a proper look at the lease, but I'm sure Edward will have made sure it's watertight. Who else lives in the building?"

"The top flat's been empty since old Mrs. Lindsay died," I replied. "She was another of his patients. I should think it would need quite a bit of doing to it to make it habitable. I mean, Mrs. Lindsay was ninety-two, and I don't think it had been even decorated for twenty years! Anyway, I imagine he purposely didn't let it again if he had all this in mind. Then, the middle flat is where Mrs. Wheatley lives, and we've seen how he's managed to get round her! Can you finish off those veg?"

Michael spooned cauliflower abstractedly onto his plate, dribbling cheese sauce onto the tablecloth in the process.

"So all that stands between Dr. Cowley and his grand schemes," he said thoughtfully, "is poor old Miss Graham."

"Oh, dear," I said, dabbing ineffectually at the

mark with my table napkin. "When you put it like that, it does sound rather sinister."

"Well, a landlord can make life quite difficult for a tenant, if he wants to."

"You mean ferocious Alsatian dogs and loud music and things?" I said. "Surely not here in Taviscombe!"

"No, I didn't mean that exactly, but didn't you say he's her doctor? That could be awkward."

"Oh, she could go to another doctor. That would be no problem. I'm sure Dr. Macdonald would take her."

"Yes, well, there are other things—repairs, outside decorations, stuff like that."

"Oh, dear," I said sadly. "If he's going to make things miserable for her, then she might not want to stay, even if she's legally entitled. It really isn't *fair*!"

"Well, we'll take it a step at a time," Michael replied. "A letter saying she's taking legal advice to kick off with, that might hold him for a while. Then, if we have to, the full legal bit."

"Can you be an angel and draft something for her to send?"

Michael is a good-hearted boy and, like his father, anxious to make sure that the meek don't get pushed around too much while they're waiting to inherit the earth.

"Okay. I'll do it after supper. What's for pudding?"

* * *

I TOOK THE LETTER round to Miss Graham the next morning.

"Oh, my dear, that *is* kind! Please thank him so much from me. Now just let me find my glasses."

"Let me know as soon as you hear from Dr. Cowley, won't you?" I said. "Then we'll see where we go from there. I can't promise that it will work out, because although I'm sure you have a legal right to stay on here, he might be able to make life quite disagreeable for you."

Miss Graham set her mouth in a firm line.

"We'll see about that!" she said. "He needn't think he can frighten me, even if he *is* a doctor!"

Slightly confused by this nonsequitur, I nevertheless felt that Miss Graham had the right spirit.

"My mother was a suffragette, you know," she continued. "She went to a lot of the rallies in London, *and* she was almost trampled by a police horse in Trafalgar Square—her hat was knocked to the ground—but she never let things like that put her off!"

Expressing admiration for the resolution of the late Mrs. Graham, I put the signed letter in its envelope and sealed it.

"Right, then. I'll just pop this in the post for you," I said.

As I was putting the letter in the box at the end of the promenade, I happened to see Dr. Cowley getting out of his car and going into one of the retirement homes on the sea-front. He had his bag with him, so I assumed he was going to visit a patient, looking every inch the old-fashioned doctor, I thought, in his well-cut tweed suit. He was a tall man, stooping slightly now, but still brisk in his movements.

His thatch of gray hair was hidden under a tweed hat, and his rather red complexion was heightened by the strong breeze that was blowing in from the sea. As he approached the door of Harbour Court, an old lady came out. He stopped and spoke to her for a moment, bowing and raising his hat as he moved on. Although I'm the first person to deplore the decline in manners nowadays, something about the way he performed this civil action irritated me. Irrational, I know, but I somehow felt, as I always do with him, that he was consciously playing a part and expecting audience approval.

I said as much to Michael that evening.

"Well," he said, fending off the dogs, who always greet him when he comes home from work with as much enthusiasm as if he's been to Siberia and back, "you're always banging on about how nobody knows how to behave anymore. I'd have thought you'd be pleased."

"But it's sort of false with him," I replied. "Not natural good manners at all. Rosemary says the same. She says he gives her a creepy feeling. You'd better go and change before Tessa covers that good suit with hairs! Supper won't be long."

Michael, now clad in a disreputable pair of jeans

and a T-shirt emblazoned with the words The Law
Is an Ass, reverted to the subject of Dr. Cowley as
we had supper.

"I checked Miss Graham's lease today," he said.
"At least, I got Jenny to check it for me, and she
says it's absolutely watertight. So, as long as the
poor old soul can manage to hold out against Cowley's harassment, there's no reason at all why she
shouldn't stay put."

"Well, that's a relief, though I do hope she's tough
enough to stand up to him. She has got a weak
heart, and nobody is more aware of *that* than he is!"

I cut myself a piece of bread. "Who's Jenny?" I
inquired casually.

"Our new legal exec."

"How long has she been with you?"

"Oh, I don't know. About a month, I suppose."

"What's she like?"

"Oh—tallish, fairish, just a girl!"

I suppose I should be used to this sort of unsatis-
factory interchange by now. Inquisitive mothers of
grown-up sons should not complain of such treatment, I suppose; it is no more than we deserve. I
must admit to more than my fair share of curiosity
and Michael is very patient with me, but over the
years he has developed this name-rank-and-number-
only school of information to cope with the aggrava-
tion. I have discussed this technique with some of
my friends, and they all agree that boys (as opposed
to girls) favor the "Where have you been?" "Out,"

"What did you do?" "Nothing," approach. Mind you, I can still remember from my own youth how it often seemed just too much trouble to attempt any communication with the older generation.

As I said to Rosemary the other day, it's not that I'm a matchmaking mother—heaven forbid—and anyway, he's far too young to settle down, but I naturally take an interest in any female friends he may make. Rosemary said, "Yes, dear," in that sardonic way that she has, and we both laughed. I realize I'm very lucky that Michael is so good-natured and allows me to fuss over him as much as he does.

Actually, I was able to see this new girl for myself a few days later. Michael rang to say he'd left a file at home and asked me to bring it in for him when I was shopping. I always feel a little strange nowadays going into what used to be Peter's offices. Edward is a dear soul, and I know Peter was glad when he took over the practice, and he was very good during that last year when Peter was so ill, but still . . . I was so pleased when Edward took Michael on as an articled clerk and I think there'll be a future for him there, which would have made Peter very happy. I had a little chat with Josie, the receptionist, who was there in Peter's time, and I was just giving her the file when another girl came into the outer office.

"Oh, here's Miss Drummond, our new legal exec. She'll take it through." Jennifer Drummond was indeed tall and fair, as Michael had said. What he hadn't mentioned was that she was extremely good-looking—not conventionally pretty (she was too tall for that) but with handsome features, a perfect complexion, and a bell of thick, tawny hair. Josie introduced us, and we made a little polite conversation about how long she had been in Taviscombe (three months) and how she liked it here (very much, especially after Wolverhampton). She had a pleasant manner and a delightful smile that lit up her face, and I liked her at once.

"You didn't tell me that your Jenny Drummond was pure Pre-Raphaelite," I said to Michael that evening.

"Oh, you saw her, did you?" he replied. "I suppose she is a bit."

"That short upper lip and the heavy mass of hair, just like a Rossetti!"

"Don't get carried away, Ma. She's a perfectly ordinary girl."

"What does she do out of office hours?" I inquired casually.

"I see her at the badminton club sometimes, but I think she's got a boyfriend because she doesn't turn up every week." He grinned. "So, no, she wouldn't 'do' for me, if that's what you're thinking."

"Well," I replied defensively, "she seemed rather a nice girl, and I thought she might be lonely, not knowing anyone here . . ."

"I know just what you thought," Michael said.

"I'm not trying to interfere," I said. "Well, not exactly—it's just that—oh, you know how I am!"

"Indeed I do. And aren't you lucky I'm such a nice, patient son who's prepared to put up with it? Besides, dearest mama," he continued, patting me on the head as he went by, you are a source of continuous entertainment, and I can't imagine what I would do without you!"

· 3 ·

A few weeks later I was on my way to call on Miss Graham, when I ran into Mrs. Wheatley, as she was coming out of the gate of Kimberley Lodge. As usual, she was smartly dressed: a cream linen suit with a pink chiffon blouse, high-heeled sandals, and a small pink hat perched on what was obviously newly set hair. I wondered if all this elegance was just for shopping in the town or if she was meeting someone—Dr. Cowley, for instance.

"Hello, Mrs. Wheatley," I greeted her, forcing her to stop and talk, though she had been prepared simply to acknowledge me and pass on.

"Isn't it a lovely day? And don't you look summery in those colors!"

She smiled faintly and said, "How kind."

"I'm just going to see Miss Graham," I went on. "She's very worried about a letter she's had from

Dr. Cowley about having to move. Have you had one, too?"

She looked flustered and spoke disjointedly.

"Well, yes, in a way—only nothing's definite, I believe—there's some complication—so I don't feel Miss Graham should be worried—I'm sure that is the last thing that Dr. Cowley would wish . . ."

I let her flounder and her voice trailed away. I allowed a silence to fall and then I said, "Well, she *is* very upset. Still, she has good friends who won't let her be harassed."

"Oh, I'm sure that's the last thing . . . ," she repeated.

We stood in silence again, and then Mrs. Wheatley said, "Do forgive me if I run now. I have an appointment."

"Of course," I said. "I mustn't keep you. By the way," I asked, intending to leave the conversation on a lighter note, "how's your little dog?"

"Oh, poor little Mitzi. I had to have her put to sleep, I'm afraid. Her *bowels*," she dropped her voice on the word, "were not reliable. I couldn't cope with the mess; it was becoming rather a nuisance—you know how it is."

"INDEED WE DO KNOW how it is!" Rosemary said when I told her of this conversation. "For heaven's sake! What a dreadful woman!"

Rosemary, like me, has nursed old, blind, deaf, and incontinent dogs and cats with love and devotion over the years. It would never occur to either of us to have them put down while there was even a flicker of enjoyment left in their lives.

"A nuisance! I suppose she thought cleaning up a few messes would spoil her *nail varnish*," she said with infinite scorn.

"I must say, I was surprised," I said. "I thought she was fond of the poor little thing."

"I expect she's one of those women who regard dogs—poodles, especially, don't you think—as sort of fashion accessories," Rosemary continued.

"She always *seemed* quite nice," I said. "Perhaps it's Dr. Cowley's dire influence."

"What do we know about her anyway?" Rosemary demanded. "What about *Mr.* Wheatley?"

"I'm sure someone said she's divorced—she *looks* divorced somehow, don't you think?—and then there was all that business about her being a kept woman and the man who visits her sometimes."

"Hmm." Rosemary considered this. "Does Miss Graham know anything about her? I mean, if this Wheatley woman is in league with Dr. Cowley and is actually living in the same house—well!"

"Well, what?" I asked.

"Well—she might be his *spy* or maybe she'll try to persuade Miss Graham to give in to his terms. Anything!"

"Miss Graham's never said very much," I said, "beyond being pleased to have such a quiet and pleasant neighbor. I don't think they're particularly friendly. I mean, I don't imagine Mrs. Wheatley drops in for coffee or anything—I don't see her as a dropper-in, anyway. No, the subject hasn't really cropped up. What Miss Graham likes most is to talk about Taviscombe in the old days, and that's liable to be a bit repetitive."

"Oh, Lord, don't I know! Mother drives me mad sometimes! And her memory! Down to the last second cousin twice removed of every man, woman, and child in the town!"

"You must admit," I said, laughing, "she does have an intelligence network second to none. I really don't know how she does it, especially now that she doesn't go out so much."

"Ah, but she goes to all the *relevant* things: the Conservative Ladies lunch, the Arts Society meetings, the W.I., and carefully selected coffee mornings. And, of course, all her old cronies come to her, thanks to Elsie's cooking—little lunch parties and tea, of course, and each one brings some little scrap of gossip. They know what they've been invited for!"

"Well," I said, "do see if any of them can shed some light on Mrs. Wheatley's past."

ONE OF MY LEAST FAVORITE THINGS is turning out the kitchen cupboards. I'm a dreadful impulse shopper where tinned food is concerned, and supermarket shelves (especially those devoted to exotica) are my downfall. Litchis, artichoke hearts, and black-eyed beans all magically find their way into my trolley, along with jars of special satay sauce, lemongrass and ginger marinades, and Mexican chili so hot I'd never dare even to open the jar. These purchases, pushed to the back of the cupboard by the more mundane tins of baked beans, sweet corn, and pineapple chunks that form a greater part of our everyday living, sit there sulking and unused for months—even years—until I finally face the fact that I'm never going to make that exciting Thai curry or stuff a taco shell, and nerve myself to throw them away.

I wiped the sticky reminder of a jar of tomato puree from one of the shelves, resolutely threw into the bin an unlabeled jar of unidentifiable dried herbs, and then crouched down on the floor to tackle the worst of the tins. Several of them appeared to have been leaking. A repulsive damp brown stain, quite impossible to wipe away, disfigured the shelf, probably for all time—and when I lifted up one of the tins (green figs in syrup) it came away with an ominous sucking sound. I was just rinsing the brown goo from my hands when the phone rang. It was Rosemary.

"It's started," she said breathlessly. "Jilly's in the hospital and Roger's having to stay at home with Delia until I get there, so I've got to go at once. Do you think you could *possibly* fetch Jack's dinner jacket from the cleaners for me—I'm sure Sandra will let you have it without the ticket. He's in

Bridgewater most of today, and he'll need it for the Rotary do tomorrow. I'll leave a message for him to pick it up from you. Is that okay?"

"Yes, of course," I replied. "And, look, tell Jack to come and have supper with us this evening, why don't you. We'd love to see him."

"Oh, bless you, that would be a help—I was going to make him get fish-and-chips or something, but he's so *helpless*. He never knows what to ask for and ends up with a hundred-weight of chips and raging indigestion!"

I've known Jack all my life; he and Rosemary and I went to the County school together, and he's a dear and faithful friend. He is, however, a person of very strong views on both people and situations, which he is liable to express with great vehemence. Fortunately both Michael and I are used to his ferocious manner and are fully aware that under that fiery exterior he's a perfect lamb.

Jack is one of our local councillors, something that Rosemary is always complaining about. "Honestly, it really is too bad! As if he hadn't enough to do working all the hours God sends so that I hardly ever see him, and then having to waste hours on this *wretched* council—a dreadful lot of pompous idiots or people who're just there to help their businesses along—you know who I mean! Always putting up grandiose schemes to increase their own self-importance, and poor old Jack, who's only there from a sense of duty, is always the one who has to bring them down to earth, and, as you can imagine, he never gets thanked for it! I tell him, you'd be much better off staying at home watching *Coronation Street*."

This evening Jack was fulminating against several of his fellow council members.

"That old idiot Roberts," he said, crunching a handful of peanuts as violently as though they were the bones of his adversary. "You'll never guess what damn-fool scheme he's putting forward now."

"I can't imagine," I said.

"He's only suggesting that we let that man— what's his name—put his godawful clock golf course at the end of the Promenade, on the cliff walk!"

"But surely that land was left to the town as an open space," I protested, "by old Colonel Lumm."

"Exactly!" Jack took a reviving pull at his whisky and went on. "That's what I told them, but apparently there's some way they can get round it—I don't know what the law is coming to, if they can do a thing like that. What do you have to say about *that*, young man?" He turned to Michael.

"It depends on the way the bequest was phrased, I'm afraid," Michael said in his best legal manner. "Apparently the land was left to the council to be used as they thought best for the benefit of the town. I suppose they *could* say that the rent they could get for it from this man would help the general finances."

"That's the sort of rot they've been telling me,"

Jack said. "Bloody fools of lawyers! The poor old Colonel must be turning in his grave!"

"It will be awful if they do take it away as an open space," I said. "It's one of the few places left where a lone female can safely take her dog for a walk, now that we're not allowed on the beach in the summer!"

"Have they got planning permission?" Michael asked.

"No, and they're not going to," Jack said grimly. "I think I've got a majority on the planning committee to oppose it, though *they're* not very sound. Take that doctor fellow and his nursing home, for instance. We turned down flat the first application he made, but then I suppose he must have got at some of the committee because he got it through the second time. Bloody nonsense. Too many nursing homes in the town, if you ask me. A lot of damned geriatrics everywhere!"

"Do you mean Dr. Cowley?" I asked.

"Yes, that's the fellow. Can't stand him myself, but all the old ladies seem to think he's the cat's whiskers."

"Oh, dear," I said, "I'm afraid he'll be badgering poor Miss Graham again, now he's got planning permission. I suppose that first refusal must have been the complication Mrs. Wheatley mentioned, but now that's cleared up he'll want to go ahead."

"What's all this about Miss Graham?" Jack demanded. "Honestly, you and Rosemary are as bad as each other for going off on a tangent so I never know *what* you're talking about!"

"Michael will explain," I said, "while I go and see to the food. Help yourself to another drink."

As I mashed butter into the potatoes, I thought about what Jack had said and decided that I'd better go and see Miss Graham quite soon. With the planning permission settled, I couldn't believe that Dr. Cowley would be content simply to wait until Miss Graham had a change of heart. She was a determined old soul once she'd made up her mind about anything, but she *was* old and she'd need all the support we could give her if she was to hold out against such a devious opponent.

"NO, MY DEAR," Miss Graham said, when I called, "he hasn't written again, but I did have a visit from Mrs. Wheatley! You could have knocked me down with a feather when I saw her standing there at the door, because we've never actually *called* on each other. Well, I invited her in, of course, and you'll never believe this! She'd come to ask me if I was going to 'take up Dr. Cowley's kind offer,' which was how she put it. Did you ever hear anything like it?"

"What did you say?" I inquired.

"Well, I told her. I said this was my home and I had a perfectly good lease and I intended to stay here."

"So what did she say to that?"

Miss Graham gave a little snort of indignation. "Such nonsense! She went on about what a good offer it was and how it would be a nice little nest egg for me and that Dr. Cowley had the lease of a very nice flat in Winterfield Road that I could have for the same rent. Winterfield Road! Can you imagine it, right by that car park—cars in and out all the time, and caravans and goodness knows what in the summer!"

"Oh, dear," I said, "it sounds horrid."

"How that Mrs. Wheatley had the nerve to suggest such a thing! And I told her so. I asked her if *she* would like to live there! She got up and went after that, and good riddance. And what's Dr. Cowley offered *her* I should like to know."

I told Miss Graham what I had seen that day in the County Hotel.

"So you see, it looks as if she's going into the scheme with him."

"Well!" she said. "It just goes to show! I suppose I should have known *she* was up to no good—high heels and nail varnish at her age! I suppose she thinks she's going to trap him into marrying her if she puts money into that plan of his. And where does *her* money come from, I wonder?"

I put my tea cup—a very pretty one, decorated with pink and gold roses—down on the little table beside me and leaned forward to put my point as forcefully as possible.

"If they're both in this, it really is going to make

life rather uncomfortable for you here. Don't you think you should accept Dr. Cowley's offer—not Winterfield Road, you'd hate it there. But if he's really keen to get you out, I daresay Michael could negotiate somewhere much nicer for you, as well as the money. What do you say?"

Miss Graham shook her head.

"No, my dear. I appreciate your concern, I really do, but I'm not going to move from here, no matter what either of them do. This is my home, and I won't be bullied into giving it up."

"But . . ."

"No, my mind is made up. Let that man do his worst!"

"THERE REALLY was something *gallant* about the poor old soul," I said to Michael when I was telling him about my visit. "*J'y suis, j'y reste.* You know the kind of thing."

"I'm sure we could put pressure on Cowley to find her somewhere reasonable," Michael said. "He'll be making a packet out of this scheme, so he could easily afford a really decent place."

"I'm afraid she's simply dug her heels in now," I said. "Old people can be very stubborn when they make up their minds to something."

"I don't like to think of the poor old bat being hassled by Cowley and that Wheatley female," Michael said. "I do think we ought to try and make her see that it could be pretty uncomfortable for her. What about that nephew of hers? Couldn't he persuade her to change her mind?"

"I don't think she wants to tell him about it," I replied. "She more or less said as much—something to do with his wife not wanting him to get involved with his aunt's affairs—a sort of family coolth. You know how it is."

Still, when I was passing Ronnie's shop the next day, I did hesitate and wonder if I should go and have a word with him. But as I looked in, he was crouched on the floor, surrounded by a quantity of rejected shoes, trying to fit a pair of tan leather brogues on Phyllis Brock, a really difficult woman—as I know from our battles on the Red Cross committee—and I felt that he had troubles enough of his own at that particular moment.

SEVERAL WEEKS went by. Rosemary returned from Taunton full of excitement about her new grandson.

"They're calling him Alexander John," she said. "Isn't that nice? Jack's delighted, though they'll call him Alex. Mother's in a great huff because they didn't name him Arthur after Father, but I ask you, whoever's called 'Arthur' these days! The poor little mite would have a dreadful time at school with an old-fashioned name like that."

"Alex is splendid," I agreed. "An interesting name, solid and not too trendy—all those Jasons and Carlys—very unsuitable for old age. Though, come to that, think how peculiar to be called *Robin* when you're in your eighties!"

Rosemary poured another cup of coffee and pushed the plate of chocolate digestives vaguely in my direction.

"Oh, by the way," she said. "To take Mother's mind off the Arthur situation, I asked her if she'd managed to get the lowdown on the Wheatley woman yet, and guess what?"

"What?"

"It seems she isn't *Mrs.* Wheatley at all—not married, just called herself that."

"Good heavens!" I said. "Do tell!"

"Well," Rosemary began, taking a deep breath. "It seems that Freda Morrison's sister Olive—you know, the one who married the doctor and went to live in Bristol—knows the Wheatley family. Wheatley used to own a chain of chemist shops there, but he sold out to one of the big multiples sometime in the sixties and made absolutely *pots* of money. Anyway, he took up with this woman, Eileen Watson—apparently she managed one of his shops—and *he* bought her the flat at Kimberley Lodge, so that he could visit her discreetly. He was a big noise on the committees of various charities by then, so he couldn't live with her openly."

"How splendidly old-fashioned!" I exclaimed. "It sounds like something out of an Edwardian novel!"

"Well, he was almost that generation—much older than her. Anyway, he died last year and left her quite a large sum of money. The family was *furious,* Freda said—well, you can imagine—but there was nothing they could do about it."

"Lots of money!" In my excitement I took another chocolate digestive and bit into it. "No wonder Dr. Cowley was smarming around her with offers of cruises and so forth."

"Trying," Rosemary said, "to persuade her to put it into that nursing home of his. I can just see him!"

We sat and looked at each other for a moment, delighted at having put together this jigsaw of cause and effect, and then I said, "Well, haven't I always said that wherever you come from, and whatever your past history, there'll always be *someone* in Taviscombe who knows someone who knows all about it! Especially," I added with feeling, "your mother."

I TOLD Miss Graham about Mrs. Wheatley's inheritance.

"Fancy that!" She sighed. "It must be nice to have money. Now if only I could have afforded to *buy* this flat, it would all have been so different. But, of course, I had to look after Mother for all those years, and then, when she passed on, I sold the house and used the money to buy the lease of that little wool shop in the Parade. It was something I'd always wanted to do. I like knitting—I was really quite an expert knitter, everyone used to say—and I *did* enjoy it. Well, you remember how cozy it used to be, people dropping in for a chat and asking me about new patterns and things. But I'm afraid I didn't really have a head for business. I never seemed to get the books to balance properly, and there was no one to advise me, and, with a wool shop, you have to put wool away for people and then they don't always come back for it, and there it is, left on your hands when you need the cash to buy new stock . . ."

Her voice trailed away, and we sat in silence for a moment. I remembered the particular atmosphere of Miss Graham's wool shop, small and overstocked, a cheerful place, though, with the fixtures stuffed full of brightly colored wools—soft lamb's wool, delicate mohair, and angora, all crying out to be touched—tottering piles of pattern books, swinging racks of needles and crochet hooks, hand-knitted garments and toys hopefully displayed, and usually two or three women deep in conversation, filling up the tiny space so that it was almost impossible to get to the counter to make a purchase.

I had heard the saga of its decline many times, how gradually the profits had got less and less, until they had finally dried up altogether and Miss Graham had been obliged to sell the remainder of the lease for quite a small sum, certainly not enough to buy any sort of flat.

"Mother and I didn't have a lot of money when Father died," she went on, "just his pension from the bank. And of course that died with Mother. Her family were farmers, over Wellington way, quite prosperous, but they didn't really approve of Father, so we never had much to do with them. I think my brother John, Ronnie's father, that is,—he died just after the war if you remember—he used to see them sometimes, but I never did." She sighed again. "Oh, well, that's all water under the bridge now, I suppose. Let's have a nice cup of tea to go with some of that lovely fruitcake you brought me."

I HAD a nagging tooth—well, it wasn't really the tooth that was aching but a sort of gum abscess that came and went. I kept waking up in the night and taking an aspirin, but by the morning I knew I'd have to go to the dentist and have it seen to. Mr. Flecker is very good about fitting you in if you're in pain, and his receptionist offered me an appointment that morning. Of course, as always, the moment I approached the surgery the pain eased off, but I knew from bitter experience that if I turned 'round and went away it would come back, worse than ever.

I always get to places too soon, so I had quite a while to wait. I sat, leafing through the pages of *The Lady* and wondering if perhaps I might take on a new career as a resident companion—"no nursing, no housework, own flat, use of car"; so different from the days of the downtrodden poor relation or the Victorian governess. I was so occupied, wondering how Jane Eyre would have responded to her own TV and use of car, that I barely noticed another patient coming into the waiting room. However, when she leaned forward to pick up a magazine from the table, I recognized the tawny hair and realized that it was Jennifer Drummond. "Hello!" I said brightly. "How are you? Nothing horrid to be done, I hope?"

She looked puzzled, obviously not recognizing me. "I'm Sheila Malory," I went on, "Michael's mother. We met briefly in your office."

"Of course!" She smiled. "How awful of me not to recognize you."

"Oh, I *never* recognize people if they suddenly appear in a place I don't expect them. It took me *ages* to identify one of the girls in the library, who I sometimes see out walking her dog. You know the face, but . . ."

"It's even worse with clients," she agreed. "They get very hurt if you pass them in the street—even if you've only seen them briefly, just the once!"

We chatted for a while, and I was pleased to see that my first impression had been right. She was a lively, intelligent girl.

"Have you settled in all right?" I asked.

"I was lucky," she said. "I managed to get a nice flat overlooking Jubilee Gardens. It's very pleasant there."

"And have you made any friends? Or did you know anyone in Taviscombe before you came?"

"No, but people have been very kind—people in the office, I mean. And I've joined a few clubs, ten-

nis and badminton and the natural history society—
I like bird-watching—and I've met a few people
that way."

"You must come and have supper with us one
evening," I said.

"Oh, that would be lovely! Thank you so much."

She sounded genuinely pleased and so, on an impulse, I said, "Can you manage this week
sometime?"

We both fished out our diaries and arranged a
date.

As I sat in the dentist's chair, tilted rather too far
back for comfort, I began to wonder if I'd done the
right thing, if Michael would think I was matchmaking and be annoyed. But then Mr. Flecker's voice
broke in on my thoughts, exhorting me to "have
a rinse away," and I concentrated on the matter
at hand.

Actually, Michael sounded quite pleased when I
told him about the invitation.

"Oh, good, she's a jolly girl, nice and cheerful,
never sulks or gets in a huff, *not* like some of them."

"Did you discover if there is a boyfriend?" I asked.
"You said you thought there might be."

"There are no obvious signs, and she never seems
to mind working late and isn't always rushing off at
lunchtime to go shopping or have her hair done."

I agreed that those were indications of a possible relationship.

"She doesn't share her flat with anyone?"

"Well, the mortgage is in her name—I helped with the conveyancing—and she always says 'I' and not 'we' when she talks about decorating and stuff like that. There now, does that satisfy your appalling curiosity?"

JENNY CAME to supper, and it was a great success. She and Michael seemed to develop a nice, easy relationship, and there were lots of little legal jokes and capping of stories about eccentric clients ("He stole this *pig* and kept it in his garage") and embarrassing situations in court ("And I suddenly realized I'd left the further and better particulars in the taxi!"). I was really pleased to see Michael so cheerful again, because his last girlfriend—a rather difficult girl called Helen, whom I wasn't, quite frankly, sorry to see the last of—had gone to New Zealand with her parents, and he'd been rather moping around for the last few months.

"IT'S NO EARTHLY USE *planning* anything for them, though," Rosemary said, when I told her how pleased I was and what a nice girl Jenny was. "When I think of all the trouble I went to over Jeremy Gardner, having him to supper, playing bridge with his boring parents, the lot! But Jilly wouldn't look at him—that was when she was absolutely besotted with that dreadful Paul Empson—the Hell's Angel, Jack used to call him—hair down to his waist, dressed in black leather, and riding that fearful mo-

torbike! Still, she found Roger in the end, so everything turned out for the best."

"I saw Paul Empson the other day," I said,
"wheeling a baby in a pushchair. He was with Jean
Armstrong's daughter, and his hair was quite short
and he was wearing a blue anorak."

"Well, there you are," Rosemary said obscurely.
"It just goes to show!"

· 4 ·

Michael went off to spend two weeks in Italy with his friend Gerry, and after he got back, I visited my cousin Joan in Kirkby Lonsdale, and then, quite suddenly, it was autumn. The summer visitors in their pink and purple shell-suits were replaced by more soberly clad pensioners on weekend bargain breaks, and the queues at the supermarkets dwindled to bearable proportions. The children went back to school, and it was possible once again to walk along the pavements of Taviscombe without being mown down by racing skateboarders or small crash-helmeted figures on junior mountain bikes.

There had been a glut of plums and I'd put quite a few in the freezer, intending to make jam with them when I had the time. Plum jam is tedious to make—all that business taking out the stones—and I'd rather put the whole thing off. However, a Monday morning, start of a new week, seemed a good moment to get down to it, and I'd just got the large preserving pan full of jam simmering on the stove when the phone rang. It was Miss Graham at her most agitated.

"Oh, Sheila, dear, I do hope I haven't rung at an inconvenient moment, but I wonder if you could possibly come round to see me sometime. There's something I want to talk to you about."

I wiped a sticky fingerprint off the phone with my apron and said, "Yes, of course. Would this afternoon be okay? I've got to go into town anyway to take some books back to the library, so I could easily call in."

"Oh, that *would* be good of you."

She sounded disproportionally relieved, and I wondered if something serious had happened. "Is anything the matter?" I asked. "Is it something to do with Dr. Cowley?"

She wasn't very coherent. "Well, it's rather unexpected, such a strange thing! I'd no idea—quite out of the *blue*, you might say . . ." She broke off. "Oh, dear, there's someone at the door—I'll tell you all about it this afternoon."

"All right. About two-thirty, I expect."

"Thank you so much, Sheila. I *am* grateful. Good-bye."

As I put the phone down, wondering what on earth could have made her so flustered, I was aware of an ominous smell of burning. I dashed into the kitchen to find that the jam had boiled over onto the top of the stove. Scraping burned-on plum jam from a ceramic hob with a kitchen knife is *not* my favorite way of spending a morning, and I felt an unreasonable resentment against Miss Graham. Still, after I—and the jam—had cooled down, I began to wonder what it was that had perturbed her so much. After lunch I put a pot of the jam into my shopping bag, rounded up the dogs and put them in the car so that I could take them for a walk on the beach after I'd been to see Miss Graham, and set out for Kimberley Lodge.

I rang the bell and huddled in the glass porch while I waited for Miss Graham to answer it. There was a strong wind blowing in off the sea, and, in spite of the bright sunlight, it was very cold. I shivered and rang the bell again. Still no one answered. Feeling rather foolish, I peered in through the flap of the mail drop. The empty hall looked quite normal. I called out, "Miss Graham! Are you there? Are you all right?" but there was no reply. It was impossible that she would have gone out; she knew I was coming and had been so anxious to see me. I began to feel worried—it seemed that something must have happened to her.

The entrance to Mrs. Wheatley's flat, which was on the second floor, was up an outside staircase. I went up and rang her bell. Again, there was no reply. I went down and rang Miss Graham's bell once more, realizing as I did so that it was a totally futile gesture, but not knowing what else to do. Everything was very still; the only sound was the hoarse cry of a sea gull circling the beach below. Kimberley Lodge stood well back from the road on its own grounds, and not a lot of traffic passed that way.

Suddenly I remembered Miss Graham telling me once that she always hid a spare key in the soil of the wooden tub that housed a bay tree by the front door. She'd been very pleased with the ingenuity of her hiding place. "I'm afraid I have got a little forgetful these days, and on several occasions I left my keys on the kitchen table and locked myself out, and that was *very* awkward! So I thought it would be a good idea to keep a spare one there, just in case!"

I took a pencil from my bag and scrabbled about in the earth of the tub. Sure enough, there was a key and it opened the front door. I stepped into the hall, feeling awkward and apprehensive.

"Miss Graham!" I called. "Are you there? It's me, Sheila."

The silence in the flat seemed a very palpable thing, oppressive and unnerving, and I had to make a real effort to move forward and open the sitting-room door. After the cold wind outside, it was pleasantly warm and the flames of the gas fire flickered cozily. Miss Graham was sitting in her usual chair by the fire. Her eyes were shut and she seemed to be sleeping. I went over to her and said, "Miss Graham, it's Sheila. Are you all right?" but somehow I knew she wouldn't reply—there was a feeling of emptiness, as if I were the only person in the room, talking to myself.

I moved toward her and, remembering my Red Cross classes, felt for the pulse in her neck, but there was no movement. I took out my handbag mirror and, kneeling down beside her chair, held it to her lips, but the glass was not even faintly misted. When I touched her face, the skin felt slightly chill and clammy and I knew that she was dead.

As I got stiffly to my feet my knees felt wet, but there was nothing to be seen on the carpet, which was fawn, patterned with large, dark brown spirals. I bent down and touched the place beside the chair and it was wet, though with what I couldn't tell. The shock suddenly got to me, and I sat down quite abruptly on the sofa facing the fire. I was shaking, and I suppose it must have taken me a good ten minutes before I got hold of myself and thought about what I had to do.

I went into the hall and found Miss Graham's address book by the telephone, looked up Dr. Cowley's number, and rang the surgery. His receptionist, a nice middle-aged woman who I knew slightly from the W.I., answered.

"Oh, hello, Miss Watson, it's Sheila Malory here. I wonder if Dr. Cowley could come round to Miss Graham's, you know, at Kimberley Lodge. I'm afraid she's—she's died."

"Oh, dear," the voice at the other end of the line sounded distressed. "Dr. Cowley *will* be upset. But

I'm afraid Monday's his day for the Dulverton surgery and he isn't usually back until quite late. Dr. Barton always covers for Dr. Cowley on his Dulverton days and he's actually here in the surgery now, so perhaps I'd better ask *him* to go round to Kimberley Lodge. Are you there yourself? Can you let him in?"

"Oh, yes, please, that would be best." I was relieved that I would not have to face Dr. Cowley in these circumstances. "And, yes, I'm in Miss Graham's flat—actually, I found her. It was quite a shock."

"Oh, that must have been most unpleasant for you! Don't you worry, Mrs. Malory. I'll send him round right away."

While I was by the telephone, it occurred to me that I should ring Miss Graham's nephew, Ronnie. As her only close relative, he ought to be told at once. I found the number of the shop, and after a while a girl's voice answered.

"Can I speak to Mr. Graham, please," I said.

"I'm sorry, he's not in today," she said. "May I take a message?"

"It's really very urgent," I persisted. "Do you know where I can get in touch with him?"

"Well, actually," the girl's interest was aroused and she sounded more animated, "he's got this flu thing that's going about, and he's at home. You should be able to get him there." She gave me the number, and then I suddenly thought of something.

"Perhaps I could speak to *Mrs.* Graham," I said, "to save bothering him when he's not well."

"Oh, *she's* gone to Taunton to see one of our suppliers—she won't be back this afternoon."

I thanked the girl and dialed Ronnie's home number. The phone rang but there was no reply; presumably he was in bed, and it seemed rather unkind to make him get up when he was feeling rotten just to hear upsetting news. I decided to wait until later when Carol would be home, and put down the receiver.

The silence closed round me again, and I began to walk about the flat simply to create some kind of movement. Consciously I avoided the sitting room—I didn't feel I could face the still figure by the fire. I opened the door of the bedroom and looked inside. Everything was immaculately tidy. Even in her eighties and hampered by ill health, Miss Graham kept up the standard of housekeeping that she had evidently learned from her rather formidable mother. The bed was covered with a fine patchwork quilt (I remembered Miss Graham working on it over the years). The dressing table, with its embroidered mats, was free of any cosmetics and held only a silver-backed brush and mirror, a photograph of old Mrs. Graham, a bottle of Yardley's lavender water, and an old-fashioned ring tree. There were a kettle and a tea tray by the bed, a book (*Rebecca* by Daphne du Maurier) and a bottle of tablets. I wandered out into the kitchen. Here, too, everything was spick-and-span. The work surfaces were clear except for matching storage containers and a wooden bread bin, so unlike my own clutter of jars, half-empty packets, and old cat and dog dishes! The sink was spotless, the dishcloth wrung out and carefully spread over the taps, and a washed cup, saucer, and plate upended to dry on the draining board. A sudden humming noise made me jump, but it was just the motor of the refrigerator starting up. While I was still in this nervous state the front door bell rang, and I greeted Dr. Barton rather incoherently. He stared at me curiously as I haltingly explained how I had let myself into the flat and had found Miss Graham dead.

I've known Dr. Barton for years. He was one of Peter's clients but neither of us liked him very much, since he is an austere, humorless man with a precise manner. He's as well known in the town for his finicky obsession with detail, with a meticulous adherence to the last letter of the law, as he is for his meanness and love of money. It was presumably the latter which had brought him in to cover for Dr. Cowley, a man whom he personally disliked and whose methods he had been known to criticize. Glad though I was not to have had to face the oleaginous Dr. Cowley in this distressing situation, I felt chilled and repelled by the sight of Dr. Barton's gaunt figure and severe manner.

He cut short my disjointed remarks with a terse,

"Yes, yes," and going toward the sitting room said, "She's in here, is she?"

I followed him in reluctantly.

"Has that fire been on for long?" he asked me sharply.

"I don't know," I replied. "It was on when I got here and the room was quite warm then."

He moved across and felt for the pulse as I had and then laid his hand on her forehead.

"Difficult to tell how long she's been dead, since the room is so warm."

He looked at me accusingly, as if it was somehow my fault.

"She was alive this morning," I said. "She telephoned to ask if I'd come and see her."

"Yes. Right." Dr. Barton began examining the body, so I went out into the kitchen again and wandered aimlessly about, peering into the refrigerator (almost empty), opening and shutting drawers (splendidly tidy), turning a dripping tap off more tightly, and generally fidgeting about until Dr. Barton called to me from the sitting room.

"Mrs. Malory," he said as I went into the room, "do you know if Miss Graham had seen Dr. Cowley in the last few days?"

"I don't know," I answered. "I shouldn't think so—I mean, she hadn't been ill or anything. She sounded perfectly all right this morning. I suppose it was a heart attack?"

"That I am not in a position to say," he replied

reprovingly. "But if she had not seen her general practitioner within the last forty-eight hours, then there will have to be a postmortem."

He spoke with a certain grim satisfaction, as if he was delighted that Dr. Cowley would be inconvenienced by the bureaucratic process.

"There is no need for you to remain," he continued. "No doubt you have things you wish to attend to. I will do all that is necessary here."

"Oh, well, thank you, that would be kind—I've got the dogs outside and they'll be getting a bit restless. You know how it is . . ."

My voice trailed away in the face of his barely concealed contempt for people who kept animals, and I picked up my handbag and shopping bag, in the bottom of which the now unneeded pot of jam rolled about forlornly, and prepared to leave.

"Just one more thing," Dr. Barton said. "Are there any relatives?"

"Just a nephew," I replied. "I tried to ring him while I was waiting for you, but he's got flu. I'll try again this evening when his wife's in.

"He should be informed. Thank you, Mrs. Malory."

Thus dismissed, I made my way slowly out of the flat. The air struck cold, but I welcomed the boisterousness of the wind as something positive and alive. I was shaken and upset, finding poor Miss Graham like that, and chilled by Dr. Barton's bleakness and lack of warmth and human sympathy. As I approached the car the two dogs started to bark, and when I opened the door they greeted me with a frenzied excitement that suddenly brought tears to my eyes. I drove down to the seafront, and we all three ran like mad things as fast as we could along the beach.

· 5 ·

The next day, the wind had dropped, but a mist had rolled in from the sea and there was low cloud on the hills, both of them apparently meeting over my cottage. I sat watching the water dripping from the thatch with Rosemary, who had come over to cheer me up after I had telephoned to tell her about Miss Graham.

"What a perfectly beastly thing for you," she said, biting into a chocolate wafer biscuit (we had both decided that a bit of comfort eating was called for), "discovering her like that. Such a shock!"

"It was rather awful," I replied. "I mean, I realized that something was wrong when I didn't get an answer, but still . . ."

"I suppose it was her heart," Rosemary continued.

"Well, that's what I said to Dr. Barton, but he wouldn't commit himself."

"He wouldn't!" Rosemary said emphatically. "He's

fearfully persnickety and cautious—everything has to be done exactly by the book. Mind you, he's a marvelous doctor; Jack's father used to have him and he pulled him through that first stroke wonderfully well."

"I was rather surprised that he covers for Dr. Cowley," I said. "I rather gathered they don't get on."

"Oh, well, Dr. Barton has never quite forgiven Dr. Cowley for what he said when Major Armstrong died."

"Really?"

"Apparently Dr. Cowley told Margaret Preston that he thought Dr. Barton should have had the X rays taken straightaway instead of waiting to see if the other treatment would work—very indiscreet of him; I mean, he ought to know you should never say *anything* in Taviscombe if you don't want it repeated! Of course, it got back to Dr. Barton and he was livid."

"So why does he cover for Dr. Cowley?" I asked.

"Oh, Dr. Barton's never been averse to picking up a bit more cash. You know how stingy he is."

I poured us both another cup of coffee.

"Oh, dear, I really shouldn't," Rosemary said in a half-hearted sort of way. "Well, one thing's for sure, with poor Miss Graham out of the way, Dr. Cowley will be able to go ahead with his plans for that nursing home."

"Yes, I suppose he will," I replied. "How infuriating. I hate to think that he's going to profit by the poor little soul's death."

"It's just as well he was in Dulverton when she died," Rosemary said. "Otherwise people might have got suspicious."

"Poor Miss Graham really was pretty upset about it all," I said. "I mean, she was going to stand up for her rights and all that, but there would have been a lot of hassle and it would all have been very unpleasant for her. Perhaps he *was* the cause of her death, worrying her into a heart attack."

"Oh, well, I don't suppose anyone could ever prove *that* in a court of law—just one more dodgy practice on Dr. Cowley's part."

"I wonder what will happen to Mrs. Wheatley now?" I said idly. "She's the last remaining obstacle to Dr. Cowley's plans, though he seems to have *that* situation well in hand. Do you think he'll marry her or what?"

"Perhaps he won't need to," Rosemary said. "Perhaps the cruise or whatever will be enough. I mean, she's been used to a fairly vague sort of relationship before, and she can afford to buy herself another flat. She may not want to marry him—*another* old man!"

"Oh, well," I said. "I certainly wouldn't waste any sympathy on her; she's a survivor if ever I saw one."

"Unlike poor Miss Graham."

We both fell silent for a while, and then Rosemary said, "Were you able to speak to Ronnie Graham?"

"Yes," I replied. "I phoned again last night. I got Carol first—very brisk, as always—but Ronnie sounded awful. He's got flu of course, but he seemed really upset about his aunt, kept going on and on about how he'll miss her. I never thought they were that close."

"Oh, you know how people are when someone dies," Rosemary said cynically. "They feel obliged to say what they think is expected of them, and Ronnie's a frightfully conventional sort of person anyway."

"Yes," I said doubtfully, "but I felt it was more than that, really genuine."

"Oh, well, perhaps it was then," Rosemary conceded. "He's a nice enough sort of person—though rather feeble I've always thought; absolutely dominated by that wife of his."

"Probably just as well," I said. "If it hadn't been for Carol's toughness and strong-mindedness, I don't suppose he'd ever have made a go of that shop. She works incredibly hard herself and expects him to do the same. They must be doing very well. 'A little gold mine,' Miss Graham used to say, and I daresay it is by now."

"I don't suppose Miss Graham had much to leave," Rosemary said, "so they won't have had any expectations there. I suppose she didn't have any other relations?"

"There were some cousins living near Wellington, I think, but no one close. Poor Miss Graham! All those years looking after her mother and then her wool shop having to close and then all this bother with Dr. Cowley at the end." I sighed. "Not a very happy life, if you come to think of it."

"Oh, I don't know," Rosemary said. "She pottered along as we all do, more or less; there weren't any great tragedies or dramas. I don't think she expected anything spectacular from life, so she probably quite enjoyed things—little things anyway, such as, people dropping in for tea and her favorite program on the telly."

I laughed. "You're right, of course. Happiness can be what you're used to, really, and things going on as they always have—well, for people like us, anyway!"

I WAS JUST TRYING to get an especially tenacious rabbit tick off Tessa's ear (spaniels are particularly prone to such things, especially if, like Tessa, they insist on trying to get their entire head down every rabbit hole they come across in a vain attempt to see if anyone's at home) when the telephone rang. Tessa, taking advantage of my loosened grip, ran off into the garden with half the tick still firmly embedded in her ear.

"Yes, hello," I said irritably, but my annoyance vanished when I heard Rosemary's excited tones.

"Sheila, I had to ring you right away—wonderful

news! Roger's been made a chief inspector and transferred to Taviscombe!"

"Oh, Rosemary, how lovely for you! Marvelous to have them all so near."

"Yes, isn't it," she replied. "Though I shall have to be particularly careful now, not to be an interfering mum; you know what I'm like!"

Rosemary is sometimes given to speaking her mind.

"Oh, Jilly will be thrilled to have you there to help with the children," I said, "especially with the new baby and everything."

"Well, it's certainly going to be a busy time for her now. They're coming to stay with us for a bit— Roger starts here at Taviscombe right away—so that they can look around for a house. And, then, of course, there'll be all the packing up to do and the move—I must help her with all that. Oh, dear," she sighed heavily. "Mother's not going to be too pleased about it all!"

"Losing her slave labor," I said. "Well, she's got Elsie after all, and Jilly and the children do come first."

"Try telling Mother that!" Rosemary said wearily. "You know what she's like."

"Is there anything I can do?" I asked.

"Oh, bless you, but I don't think—oh, actually, yes, there is. *Could* you take Mother to the Arts Society lunch next week—if you're going, that is. I know she could perfectly well get a taxi, but since it's a buffet and not a sit-down thing, she does like to have someone around doing the lady-in-waiting bit, fetching the food and finding a suitable seat and so on. I know it's a lot to ask, but . . ."

"Of course, I will," I replied. "I've got to go anyway because I'm still on the committee, fool that I am, and dancing attendance on your mama will be more entertaining than having to talk to Iris Marshall, who's been trying to get at me for ages. She wants me to 'give them a little talk about writing,' if you've ever heard anything so horrendous!"

"Oh, that's marvelous," Rosemary said enthusiastically. "It'll give me a clear run to look after the children while Jilly goes to look at a couple of houses. The Welch place is back on the market—gorgeous situation, up on the hill overlooking the sea—but they haven't been there long, so I wondered if there was something wrong with it."

"Oh, hadn't you heard?" I replied. "Frank Welch is having to move to Paignton. His firm's opening a branch down there, and he's going to manage it—Michael told me the other day—so I should think they'd be quite keen to make a quick sale."

I was delighted for Rosemary's sake that Jilly and Roger would be moving to Taviscombe, partly because I hoped Jilly might share some of the burden of old Mrs. Dudley with her mother and partly because Rosemary loves to be surrounded by young people (I wasn't quite so sure that Jack would welcome such a wholesale invasion of their house) and seems to thrive on the complicated logistics such an exercise involves. I was pleased, too. I'm very fond of them both. Jilly is my goddaughter, and I regard Roger as a sort of honorary godson. He shares my devotion to Victorian female novelists (I remember thinking this a rather odd taste in a policeman when I first met him), and we often have invigorating arguments about the respective merits of Mrs. Oliphant and Mrs. Gaskell and similar fascinating topics.

In view of this conversation, I wasn't too surprised to get a phone call from Roger a few days later.

"Hello, Roger, lovely to hear from you. Congratulations! It'll be splendid having you here! Are you phoning about the Welch house? It should suit you all very well. I know for a fact that Felicity Welch had that kitchen completely remodeled when they first moved in two years ago . . ."

"Actually, no, that wasn't why I'm ringing." Roger's voice was grave, unlike his usual cheerful tone. "I'm afraid this is an official call."

"Good heavens! What's happened? Nothing's happened to Michael?"

"No, no, nothing like that. It's Miss Graham. As you know, after she died so suddenly, there was a postmortem, and certain things about the results of *that* made it necessary to do an autopsy." He paused. "The fact is, it seems that it was not a natural death. She was murdered."

"Murdered?" I repeated stupidly. "But . . . but she

just looked . . . well, so *natural,* I suppose you'd say. I assumed it was a heart attack. *How* was she murdered?"

"Poison. Digitalis."

"Poison! How terrible!"

The memory of the still figure sitting in that silent flat suddenly swept over me, and I found that I was trembling.

"Sheila!" Roger's voice at the other end of the line was sharp with anxiety. "Sheila! Are you all right? I'm sorry. I shouldn't have told you over the phone. It was thoughtless of me."

"It's all right," I said. "It was a bit of a shock . . . having found her like that. Just a minute; I'm going to sit down."

"Look, since you found the body, you'll have to make an official statement anyway, so I'll come round later on. You go off now and make yourself a cup of tea—and put some brandy in it."

"Yes," I said. "I think I will."

While I was waiting for the kettle to boil, I tried to gather my thoughts. But, try as I might, I could think of nothing about Miss Graham or her flat that day that would have given any indication that anything was wrong.

Foss, attracted by my presence in the kitchen, suddenly materialized loudly demanding food, and as I abstractedly opened a tin for him I tried to visualize the sitting room. My memory shied away from the still figure in the armchair, but I felt again the heat of the electric fire and suddenly remembered the patch of damp beside her chair. There was something else, as well, something that I had subconsciously noted as being odd at the time, but, however hard I tried to pin it down, continued to elude me.

I felt better after the tea (though I didn't put brandy in it) and a bar of chocolate that I shared with the dogs, and when Roger arrived I was feeling much more composed.

"Hello, Sheila," he greeted me. "How are you feeling? It was stupid of me to ring like that, I suppose, but I thought, as Miss Graham was a friend of yours, I'd just let you know informally before we interviewed you officially."

"Oh, I'm glad you did," I replied. "Now that I'm over the shock, I've been able to think about it, so I may be a bit more helpful!" I rounded up the dogs, who were giving Roger their usual exuberant welcome.

"Do go into the sitting room. I'll just shut the animals in the kitchen so that we can get a bit of peace. Will you have a cup of tea or coffee or something?"

"No, thanks, but I'd love a glass of water—I've just been chairing a rather obstreperous meeting, and my throat's like sandpaper!"

When I came back into the sitting room with the water, he was standing by the window looking out at the hills beyond the garden.

"It really is a marvelous view. And aren't you lucky that no one can build in those fields? From what I've heard from Rosemary, the Welch house up on the hill has terrific views, too—right across the bay. It sounds ideal."

"Yes, it's just above Kimberley Lodge where Miss Graham lives—lived. She loved the view, too, which was why it would have been so hard for her to have had to leave it."

I told Roger about Dr. Cowley and his plans for turning Kimberley Lodge into a nursing home and how Miss Graham was holding out against him.

"And do you think she'd really have hung on?" Roger asked.

"Oh, yes," I replied. "Old people can be very stubborn sometimes, and that flat meant everything to her. And, after all, she did have the law on her side and lots of support from her friends."

"I see." Roger sounded thoughtful. "So this Dr. Cowley would have found it difficult to get her out."

"Oh, yes. Just as well for him that he was in Dulverton all day, else he'd have been an ideal murder suspect!"

"I gather you don't greatly care for Dr. Cowley," Roger said and laughed.

"Well, you must admit he was pretty foul to poor Miss Graham," I replied. "But it's not just that—I've never really liked him. Rosemary calls him *smarmy*, and Mrs. Dudley is quite eloquent on the subject!"

"I bet! Well, we'll investigate Dr. Cowley's movements pretty thoroughly, I can promise you that."

"Have you seen Miss Graham's nephew, Ronnie, yet?" I asked.

"Yes. I saw him first, of course, since he's the next of kin. Not that I was able to have much of a talk with him. He's got flu, and his wife would let me see him for only a short while. I must say, he did look pretty rough and he was obviously very shocked when I told him that his aunt had been murdered."

"Poor Ronnie," I said. "He's never been one to cope—I suppose Carol will be making all the funeral arrangements and so forth."

"Sheila," Roger said suddenly, "I have a favor to ask you."

"Of course," I replied, surprised at this sudden request.

"You know Taviscombe so well, the people and what goes on here—and what *has* gone on here in the past—and you know how much I value your opinion and judgment."

He paused, and I looked at him inquiringly.

"What I was going to ask," he continued, "was, can I talk things over with you from time to time—off the record? It would be a great help!"

"Of course."

"Marvelous! And there's another thing. Would you mind coming with me to Miss Graham's flat and going over what you did that day?"

"Yes, I'll do that, if you think it'll help."

"And perhaps," he hesitated, "well, you have a *feeling* for things and places. You might just be able to spot something wrong, something that isn't where it should be."

"The dog that didn't bark in the night." I smiled. "Yes, I'll certainly do that. When would you like me to come?"

"Would now be inconvenient?"

"No, I'll just change my shoes and get a coat." I picked up the empty glass to take it out to the kitchen. "Oh, Roger," I said. "Before we go, I wonder if you'd be an angel and hold Foss for me while I give him his antibiotic tablet. He does struggle so, and I forgot to ask Michael before he went to work this morning."

· 6 ·

I was glad I was with Roger as I approached Kimberley Lodge again—the memory of my last visit there was still vivid in my mind. Roger spoke briefly to the constable who was standing just inside the gate, and we went past him up the short drive.

"Now then," Roger said. "Tell me exactly what happened that day."

"Well," I said, trying to free my mind of the jumble of upsetting memories and to think coherently about the sequence of events. "I rang the bell several times, but there was no reply. I was puzzled, of course, because I knew she was expecting me. As I told you, she'd asked me to call because something unexpected had happened."

"She didn't say what it was?" Roger asked.

"No," I replied. "Just that it had happened—what was it she said?—'out of the blue.' I think it was something to do with Dr. Cowley and the trouble about the flat, but she said she'd tell me all about it when I went round."

"I see. Go on. You couldn't get her to respond, so then what?"

"I was worried in case something had happened to her—well, you know how it is with old people, you're always afraid they might have had a fall and are lying there helpless. Anyway, I remembered that she used to keep a spare key in the earth of the wooden tub by the door—the one with the bay tree growing in it. So I got that and let myself in."

"I see." Roger produced a key, opened the front door of the flat, and we went in. "What happened then?"

"I called out to her, but there was no reply, so I went into the sitting room, and there she was, sitting in her chair by the fire. I thought she was asleep."

Roger opened the door of the sitting room and went in. I followed reluctantly, but of course the chair by the fire was empty—the whole room seemed empty and cold.

"The gas fire was on?" Roger asked.

"Yes, the room was very warm."

"And she was sitting in this chair?" He indicated the fireside chair with its chintz cover (a pattern of green willow leaves on a cream ground—I remembered Miss Graham telling me with pride that it was a William Morris design) and wooden arms.

"I tried to wake her," I said slowly, "but I realized that she was dead. She looked quite peaceful, her face wasn't—there was nothing to show that she'd been . . ." I broke off.

"No, well, that particular type of poison wouldn't have left her with contorted features or anything like that."

"There was a damp patch beside her chair," I said. "I felt it when I knelt down beside her."

"Where? Show me."

I tried to find the exact spot, the brown spiral on the fawn background of the carpet.

"It would have been about here," I said, "but it's difficult to tell because the stain or whatever it was doesn't show."

Roger took some tweezers and a small plastic envelope from his pocket and pulled a few threads from the patch of carpet I had indicated.

"We'll get this analyzed," he said. "You never know."

I looked round the room, which was once so cozy but now seemed as lifeless as its owner.

"Nothing seems to be out of place or anything," I said. "Just different."

"Different?"

"Because Miss Graham isn't here," I explained. "It doesn't belong to anyone now, if you see what I mean."

"Yes, I know," Roger said, glancing round. "Right, then. Let's have a look at the other rooms."

In the bedroom he examined the kettle carefully and picked up the bottle of tablets from the table by the bed, putting it into another small plastic bag.

"She took mild sleeping tablets," I said. "She was a bit ashamed of them, actually—said that it seemed wrong to have to take something to make you sleep. Her generation never really accepted the idea of pills and tablets—Mother was the same—they thought it was somehow a sign of weakness."

Roger smiled. He went over to the wardrobe and looked inside. Then he opened the drawers of the dressing table and the small bow-fronted chest of drawers by the window. There was nothing there except Miss Graham's clothes, carefully put away and neatly folded. I turned my head away. It seemed wrong to be looking through her things like this, though I knew it had to be done. In a silly way I was glad that I was there, as if I was somehow shielding Miss Graham from the embarrassment of having a *man* (however nice and sympathetic and for whatever reason) going through her more intimate garments.

"Nothing here," Roger said. "Let's have a look at the kitchen. The pathology report said that she'd eaten breakfast—toast and marmalade and tea—and then had some sort of cake and coffee. No lunch."

"She always had lunch at twelve-thirty," I said. "Regular as clockwork."

"Good," Roger said. "That means that she was dead before then." He opened the storage jars. "Tea, sugar . . ." He reached up and opened a cupboard above the counter-top. "Instant coffee—we'd better have all these analyzed. Ah, here's a cake tin."

He lifted it down, and I saw with a pang that it was the old Harrods biscuit tin I had given her (full of biscuits) last year and which she'd kept. Using a tea cloth, presumably for fear of fingerprints, Roger took off the lid and looked inside.

"Cakes," he said.

"Let me look." I moved over quickly and stood beside him. "Little almond tartlets—I wonder who gave her those?"

"Gave?"

"Miss Graham was a dreadful cook," I explained, "but she adored cakes and biscuits, so her friends usually brought some when they visited her. Someone must have given her these."

"*She* might have bought them," he suggested.

"No, look. They're homemade and really quite fresh. They smell delicious."

I made as if to pick one up, but Roger stopped me.

"Be careful. We don't know what's in them."

I withdrew my hand as if I'd been stung.

"Goodness! How terrible! There's quite a strong almond smell," I said excitedly. "Ground almonds and quite a bit of almond essence, so the cakes would taste of it. I suppose that would have disguised anything—poison—that might have been put in them."

"True." Roger put the lid back on and wrapped the tin in the tea cloth and put it to one side.

"Perhaps she'd had someone to coffee and they brought the cakes—"

"Goodness, yes," I exclaimed. "When I was on the phone with her, the morning she died, she broke off her conversation because she said that someone was at the door!"

"What time was this?" Roger asked.

"Let me see. I started to make the plum jam at about ten-thirty." Roger looked at me in some bewilderment. "It had just reached boiling point—'a good rolling boil,' the cookery books always call it—and was simmering nicely when Miss Graham rang, so that would be about eleven o'clock."

"I see."

"And eleven o'clock," I went on, "would be the sort of time someone might come to coffee."

"But she didn't say she was expecting anyone?" Roger asked.

"No," I said. "Actually, come to think of it, I don't think she can have been—I mean she just said there was someone at the door, which isn't what you'd say if you'd invited someone."

"Right, then," Roger said. "Someone came to see her at about eleven o'clock. We know that she had coffee and cake, perhaps her visitor did, too—coffee at least, though probably not the cake—then whoever it was washed up his own cup and saucer and put it away, leaving just the one lot of crockery on the draining board so no one would know she'd had a visitor. I mean, they'd have no idea that she'd just been talking to you on the phone—"

"I know what it was!" I broke in excitedly. "I *knew* something wasn't quite right—it's been niggling away at me!"

"What is it? What's wrong?"

"Those things on the draining board," I said. "She wouldn't have left them like that."

We both turned and looked at the cup, saucer, and plate neatly upended.

"What's wrong with that?" Roger asked.

"She'd have used the dishwasher. There, look, on the other drainer."

I pointed to a small dishwasher ensconced on the right-hand draining board. "It's the dishwasher I used to have, but, when Michael came home to live after he left college, it was too small. So I got a larger one and passed this on to Miss Graham. She was very thrilled and always used it."

"I see." Roger opened the door of the little machine, and we looked inside. There was a mug, a small jug, a plate, and a cup and saucer. All of them had been used but not washed up.

"The mug would be her hot milk from last night, and the rest would be from the morning," I said. "She'd have put them in here after breakfast. She put the things in during the day as she used them and then washed the whole lot up after supper."

"Well done, Sheila!" Roger smiled at me. "I knew

that bringing you along here was a good idea! Now we can have these checked and eliminated, so we can be almost certain that the poison was in the cake or coffee she had sometime after eleven."

"And whoever murdered her thought he was being so clever," I said, "washing up the cup and things so neatly, just as they imagined *she* might have done. I don't suppose it occurred to them that an elderly person like Miss Graham would have a dishwasher, and it's not immediately obvious what it is, sitting on the draining board like that."

"Who knew about the dishwasher?" Roger asked. "I suppose her nephew would have known?"

"I expect she would have mentioned it to him," I said, "but, of course, men never really take in domestic details like that, especially from an old person like Miss Graham, who did rather go *on* about things."

"And the little cakes," Roger said. "You think someone brought them for her?"

"Oh, yes. And I'd think, wouldn't you," I went on, "that it must have been this same person, the one who tidied away the crockery?"

"It seems probable."

We stood for a moment in silence, both of us staring at the sink as if somehow it could tell us who had been there that morning.

"Beware the Greeks bearing gifts," Roger said thoughtfully. "It must have been someone who knew about her love of cakes."

"It's horrible," I said vehemently, "to bring her

something like that, something they knew she loved, and use it to poison her!"

"Murder is horrible," Roger said, "however it's done. Still I do agree that it was a particularly cynical sort of method."

I thought of how delighted Miss Graham would have been with the almond tarts: I imagined her picking one up with exclamations of pleasure, taking a bite, and tasting the almond flavoring.

"Would it have been quick?" I asked. "The poison, I mean. Would she have suffered much?"

"No, it would have been quick."

"I wonder why the murderer left the other cakes?" I asked. "Why not take them away?"

"I think you'll find," Roger said, "that the remaining cakes will be perfectly all right. I think it was just the one that was poisoned, so there would be no need to dispose of the others; they'd just be— well, cakes in a tin."

I thought about this for a moment, and then I said, "Of course, normally it would have been Dr. Cowley who'd have been called in, and he would probably just have signed the death certificate. After all, he was her doctor. And I daresay any other doctor but Dr. Barton might have done so, too—I mean, she was old and frail; it might easily have been a heart attack—or they might have waited for Dr. Cowley to see her when he got back from Dulverton. But Dr. Barton would have been delighted to put something over on Dr. Cowley—he really disliked him—and anyway, he's so persnickety and insists on doing every little thing strictly by the book! It was pure chance really that the murder came to light."

"Mmm, yes," Roger said absently. "I must let the scene-of-the-crime people loose now—fingerprints, checking the crockery and food and so on—but I wanted you to have a quick look round first before anything was disturbed. Now, I suppose I must get on and check where everyone was."

"Have you spoken to Mrs. Wheatley yet?" I asked. "She lives in the flat above."

"Yes," Roger replied. "I did have a brief word. She says she was out all morning."

"Well, I couldn't get any reply from her flat when I was trying to get in to Miss Graham," I said. "Where was she anyway?"

"Shopping, she said, just around the town. Why? Do you have any reason to think that she could have had any possible motive to kill Miss Graham? She doesn't *look* a likely suspect, on the face of it."

I told him about how Dr. Cowley's plans for a nursing home at Kimberley Lodge had included Mrs. Wheatley and what her background had been.

"Good heavens!" he said. "What extraordinary things you and Rosemary uncover when you set your minds to it—I almost feel sorry for the woman!"

"Oh, well," I said and laughed, "that's Taviscombe for you. Now you know what you're getting into now you've moved here. You'll be under the micro-scope, too."

· 7 ·

When I called for Mrs. Dudley to take her to the Arts Society lunch, she gave me one of her quick, appraising, critical looks, and I was immediately aware that I should have worn my better suit, that the collar of my blouse wasn't properly ironed, and that I was not wearing a hat. Mrs. Dudley was wearing a hat, of course, and her suit was very expensive indeed. As I helped her into the car and tucked the walking stick that she now reluctantly used in beside her, she said, "So poor little Miss Graham has got herself murdered."

She made it sound as though it was somehow Miss Graham's fault.

"Well," she continued, "they won't need to look far to find out who did *that*."

"What do you mean?" I asked.

"Dr. Cowley, of course. He needed her out of the

way for that scheme of his, so he simply *swept* her aside!"

She waved a gloved hand in a contemptuous gesture.

"I don't think it can have been him," I said. "It was his day for the Dulverton surgery."

"He may have *said* that." Mrs. Dudley was unwilling to relinquish a good suspect for a trivial little thing like a fact. "But can we believe him?"

"Well," I said, "I'm sure Roger will investigate his alibi very thoroughly."

"Yes, and that's another thing," Mrs. Dudley said, pursing her lips. "I can't say I'm particularly pleased that *he* is involved in this affair. No one in our family has ever been connected with anything like that."

"But it's his job," I said as patiently as I could. "That's what he has to do."

"I abhor violence," she went on as if I hadn't spoken. "I have always been very sensitive to that sort of thing."

This from Mrs. Dudley, who was tough as old boots.

"Now that he and Jilly will be living in Taviscombe and it is known that he is related to *me*, well, I shall expect a very high standard of behavior from both of them."

I was saved from having to comment on this by our arrival at Brunswick Lodge, where the lunch was to be held. It is a rather nice Georgian building, owned by the local council, and is used by the various cultural societies in Taviscombe for meetings, concerts, and art exhibitions. Today trestle tables ladened with a substantial buffet lunch had been set out in the main double drawing room. Mrs. Dudley surveyed the scene with a practiced eye.

"I shall go and sit at that little table by the window," she said, "and perhaps, Sheila, you will be good enough to fetch me something to eat—just a very little. You know that I have positively no appetite these days. Oh, and on your way, tell Christine Shrewsbury that I want a word with her."

Thus dismissed, I passed on her command to the hapless Christine—who groaned and said, "Oh, Lord! What have I done now!"—and made my way to the table of food. I was piling a plate high with quiche, salmon tartlets, anchovy rolls, and other goodies (I paid no attention to Mrs. Dudley's claim to a birdlike appetite, knowing just how voracious it really was), when a voice behind me said, "Don't tell me you're going to eat all that lot!"

It was my friend Sybil Jacobs.

"Goodness, no, this isn't for me. It's for Mrs. Dudley. Hang on a sec while I take it over to her— I want to ask you about what's been arranged about the concert on the twenty-ninth."

I picked up a glass of wine and took it and the plate full of food to the table by the window where Mrs. Dudley paused briefly in her harangue of the wretched Christine to acknowledge me. ("Thank you, Sheila dear, how kind. Though you know I am not allowed to eat anchovy—still, as you've brought it . . .") And I thankfully made my escape.

I made my more modest choice of food and went and sat down beside Sybil, at a table well away from the window. After we had thoroughly thrashed out the concert arrangements and dealt with the criminal inadequacy of the booking committee, Sybil said, "I was so sorry to hear about poor Miss Graham. And you found her, too. It must have been a dreadful experience."

"It was," I replied. "Perfectly horrible."

"I'm sure you coped splendidly. I shouldn't have had the least idea what to do."

"I just called her doctor."

"Oh, yes, of course, she had Dr. Cowley, didn't she? I can't stand the man—he's Pauline's doctor, you know. *She* thinks he's marvelous."

There was a wealth of scorn in Sybil's voice, but this didn't really surprise me. Pauline was her elder sister. They shared a house, and, although they were basically very fond of each other, they argued incessantly. One of them only had to hold an opinion on any subject for the other promptly to take the opposite view.

"Yes, he is," I replied, "but it was his day for going to his surgery at Dulverton, so Dr. Barton came instead."

"Oh, that man! I can't stand him, either," said Sybil, vehemently stabbing a small sausage with a cocktail stick. "He was really disagreeable when he came to see Pauline once, when Dr. Cowley was away—counting out the tablets she was to take, as if I was a complete fool who couldn't be trusted to give my own sister her medicine!"

"Oh, he's fearfully persnickety," I agreed, "and has a *very* brusque manner!"

"Hang on, though," Sybil said. "Which day was this?"

"When Miss Graham . . . when she died? It was last Monday. Why?"

"But Dr. Cowley wasn't in Dulverton then—not in the morning at any rate—because I saw him in Taviscombe."

"What!" I looked at her in amazement. "What time was this?"

"Umm. Let me see." She took a bite from a vol-au-vent. "Ugh, sardine. I loathe sardines!" She pushed the plate away and thought for a moment. "It must have been about eleven, because I had to be at the dentist at eleven, and I was late because Pauline couldn't find the books she wanted me to take back to the library, wouldn't you know! And I'd had to park the car at the bottom of West Hill, because you can never find anywhere to park outside Mr. Frobisher's."

"You mean you saw him on West Hill!" I exclaimed. "Dr. Cowley? At eleven o'clock?"

"Yes, that's right."

"Are you sure?" I persisted.

"Positive. He almost knocked me down. I was just stepping off the pavement when he came round the corner—going *much* too fast, too old to be driving, if you ask me—and sped on up West Hill. I was really quite shaken!"

"Good gracious," I said. "How odd."

"Oh, well, he is, isn't he? I said to Pauline, 'Why don't you have Dr. Mansfield, like me—such a nice young man.' I do think it's important to have a *young* doctor. It stands to reason; they're always much more up to date and know what all the latest medicines and modern treatments are. Dr. Cowley's so old-fashioned, I'm surprised he isn't still using leeches! Oh, yes, talking about old-fashioned things, I found a lovely new name the other day." Sybil and I collected odd or unusual house names, of which there's a plentiful supply in Taviscombe. "One of those little semis in Falkener Road. It's called 'Elsinore'!"

"Goodness!" I exclaimed. "What do you think their home life is like! I saw a nice one in Taunton last week; one of the terraced houses down by the station is called 'Valhalla'!"

"There's optimism for you," Sybil said and laughed. "Or would it be complacency?" She turned to put her plate on the table. "Oh, dear, I think Mrs. Dudley's beckoning you."

All the time I was dancing attendance on Mrs. Dudley, I was turning over in my mind the fact that Dr. Cowley had been in Taviscombe at just about the time Miss Graham had been murdered. Indeed, I was so abstracted that I allowed Iris Marshall to corner me and found myself agreeing to give a talk on "anything to do with literature, we leave it to you."

"I've a good mind to talk to them about some obscure modern South American novelist they've never heard of," I said viciously to Michael that evening.

"You never read modern novels, South American or otherwise," he replied. "Anyway, I'm sure you've got something tucked away in your desk that will do."

"Like Canon Chasuble's sermon on the manna in the wilderness, suitable for any occasion? Oh, I daresay I can fudge something up, but it's a nuisance. What was extraordinary was the fact that Sybil Jacobs saw Dr. Cowley in Taviscombe, actually on West Hill on the morning Miss Graham was murdered, when he was supposed to be in Dulverton."

Michael stopped winding new strapping round the handle of his badminton racket and looked up.

"The plot thickens! Are you going to tell Roger?"

"Well, I think I should, don't you?" I said.

"Of course. Go and do it now."

I looked at the clock.

"They'll still be having supper. You know Jack never gets back until after eight. I'll leave it for a bit."

I was restless, though, and couldn't settle to anything, so Foss, who had hoped for a quiet evening sitting on my lap, jumped down with a cry of annoyance and went and sat on the windowsill. There he sat lashing his tail, to the imminent danger of a rather nice rex begonia that stood in a pot there.

Michael stood up and waved the mended racket in the air experimentally.

"There, that'll have to do. I really need a new one, but they're so expensive. Oh, by the way, Ma, can I bring Jenny back for supper tomorrow? We're both playing in the quarter-finals of the tournament, and afterward is always a bit of an anticlimax."

"Yes, of course," I said, instantly diverted from thoughts of my telephone call to Roger. "What shall I get to eat?"

"Oh, anything will be fine," Michael said unhelpfully. "Right now I'm off to see if Gerry's managed to set up that clay shoot for Saturday. Won't be late."

I was glad that Michael's friendship (I supposed one might call it that) with Jenny was progressing. She seemed a nice girl and would surely divert his thoughts from the absent Helen. I wondered about the boyfriend, but perhaps that was an invention of Michael's to stop me making "plans."

When I rang through to Rosemary's, I got Roger straightaway, so I didn't have to explain why I was calling to anyone else—I wasn't sure if Roger had told the family that he was involving me, however minimally, in the investigation.

"Oh, Roger, sorry to bother you at home. But I just learned today that Dr. Cowley *was* around in the West Hill area at just about the time Miss Graham was killed."

I told him what Sybil had told me and was pleased to hear his exclamation of surprise.

"Are you sure? Is this Sybil Jacobs reliable—I mean, she couldn't be mistaken?"

"Oh, Sybil is *very* beady-eyed," I said. "Anyway, she dislikes Dr. Cowley, and you know how aware you always are of people you dislike. Anyway, he nearly ran her over, so she jolly well noticed him then!"

"And this was about eleven o'clock?" Roger asked.

"Yes, she knew the time because she was rushing to keep an appointment at the dentist. So what about Dr. Cowley? Did he say that he was in Dulverton all the time?"

"He said he took his surgery there from nine until ten and then did visits in the area," Roger said thoughtfully. "He gave me a list of patients he visited, but I haven't got around to checking them yet."

"Well, he could get back from Dulverton to Taviscombe in about forty-five minutes, I suppose. Not much less, really, because it's a narrow, winding road and you can't go fast. So that's an hour and a half traveling back and forth," I said. "Then talking to Miss Graham and doing all the business with the coffee and cakes—it would have taken most of the morning. Surely he couldn't hope to get away with such a dodgy alibi!"

"Well," Roger said, "I'll get over to Dulverton first thing tomorrow morning and check those patients and then see what Dr. Cowley has to say. Thank you, Sheila—you really do provide a marvelous information-gathering service! I'll let you know what happens."

IT WASN'T until almost teatime, when I was just putting the finishing touches to a lemon tart I was making for supper, that Roger called back.

"I checked the patients Dr. Cowley said he saw—there were only two of them. One was an old man living alone in a cottage miles from anywhere and very vague. *He* couldn't say whether Dr. Cowley came before or after lunch; he thinks it was after, but since he has it—bread and cheese, I gather—at about eleven-thirty, that wasn't much help. The other one, a woman, very deaf, said the doctor didn't come until the afternoon, but said he'd come in the morning and couldn't make her hear!"

"Oh. *Not* much help there, either! So have you seen Dr. Cowley again?"

"Well, yes," Roger replied. "But he stuck by his original story—that he went to the deaf woman at eleven o'clock, and, when he couldn't make her hear, he went back to the surgery to catch up on some paperwork and went on to see the old man at twelve o'clock."

"Did you tell him that someone had seen him in Taviscombe at eleven o'clock?" I asked.

"I did. All I could get out of him was that whoever thought they saw him was mistaken."

"So it would be Sybil's word against his?"

"I'm afraid so."

"Oh, bother. I thought we'd really got him there! But honestly, I really would trust Sybil's story rather than his. I mean, she's got nothing to gain by saying she saw him, but he's got everything to gain by denying it."

"Well, I'll certainly bear it in mind. I really don't have many leads yet. Oh, by the way, that stain on the carpet by her chair was coffee. She must have had the cup in her hand when she died and dropped it. It wouldn't have broken on the carpet, so the murderer just picked it up and washed it and put it on the draining board."

"How beastly," I said. "Horrible, calculating, and cruel."

I USED the same words later that evening when Michael and Jenny were discussing the murder over supper.

"It was such a *mean* thing to do," I said, "taking cakes as a present and poisoning her with them! The sort of thing the Borgias might have done!"

"They've definitely decided that was how she was killed, then?" Michael asked.

"Yes, Roger's had the results of the autopsy. He rang today to tell me when the inquest's to be. I shall have to go, I suppose, because of finding the body."

"She was a nice old lady," Jenny said. "I met her once when I had to take some papers for her to sign. I thought she was very sweet. She insisted on giving me tea and cake, although it was just after lunch. She said I was much too thin and needed building up—just like my grandmother!"

"I shall miss her," I said. "There aren't many of her generation left now, people my mother used to know who knew me as a child. It feels odd, somehow, to know that *you're* the older generation now!"

"That sounds very metaphysical, Ma," Michael said. "Would you like some more of that lemon tart, Jenny? No? Oh, well, I'll just finish it off then— save putting that little bit back in the fridge. Well, I suppose," he went on, scooping the last of the cream from the dish, "Dr. Cowley *has* to be the murderer. He was the only person with any possible motive, and," he said, licking the cream spoon, "if he *was* seen actually near the flat at the time of the murder—well, there you are!"

Jenny looked startled. "Was he really?" she asked. "That does seem conclusive. So what will the police do?"

"Well," I replied, "it's his word against Sybil Jacobs's—she's the person who saw him—but I suppose they'll need a bit more than that. Proof of some kind, though I don't quite know how they're going to get that, unless someone actually saw him at Kimberley Lodge."

"You didn't see anything?" Jenny asked.

"No, but then I didn't get there till the afternoon. She'd been dead for a little while then."

"It must have been awful for you," Jenny said. "Finding her like that. I've never seen anyone dead; it must be—I don't know—frightening."

"She looked quite peaceful," I replied, "but it was a dreadful shock. I've been trying not to think about it too much."

Jenny flushed and looked confused.

"I'm so sorry—it was silly of me to remind you like that."

I smiled at her. "It's all right. I'm more or less over it now. Well, now," I said, briskly getting up from the table, "you two go into the sitting room, and I'll get the coffee."

"Can I help you wash up?" Jenny asked.

"No, that's fine, I'll just stack them in the dishwasher. You go on, though."

I took quite a little time fiddling about in the kitchen—putting things away, feeding Foss and the dogs, and various little jobs that didn't really need doing, just to fill in time—but when I took the coffee into the sitting room, Michael and Jenny were simply holding a postmortem on the badminton matches they'd played that evening.

"Never mind," I told the dogs later that evening as I let them out into the garden for a last run round. "There's plenty of time—they've only known each other for a little while, and they do seem to get on very well together."

· 8 ·

"**M**a!" A plaintive voice from the kitchen arrested me when I was half way up the stairs on my way to make the beds. "Ma! Have we any proper cheese?"

Resignedly I came down again and went to see what was the matter. The countertop was covered in slices of bread, butter (now encrusted with crumbs) still in its paper, a selection of jars of pickle and a large piece of Brie, which Michael was regarding with some distaste.

"I can only find this squishy stuff," he said, "and it's no earthly good for making cheese and pickle sandwiches."

"Michael, what on earth are you doing?"

"Making *sandwiches*," he said, "or I would be if I could find the cheese."

"There's some cheddar in the other fridge in the

larder," I said, "but *why* are you making sandwiches? And do you have to make such a mess?"

"I was trying to save you the bother," he replied reproachfully.

I went into the larder to get the cheese.

"Here," I said, "let me do it. You'll cut great chunks and crumble the rest of it. Anyway," I added as I got out the cheese slicer, "what do you want sandwiches *for*?"

"I'm going bird-watching."

"Bird-watching!" I exclaimed. "Who with?"

"The naturalists. They meet every other Saturday—Jenny asked me to come the other evening. We're all meeting at Five Barrows Head—apparently there's a good chance of seeing a hobby there."

"A hobby?" I echoed.

"A bird, Ma, a kind of falcon. Jolly interesting."

"Oh, I see. It sounds very nice," I said. "I didn't know you were keen on birds."

"Well, I'm not dotty about them, like some of that naturalist lot, but it sounded quite fun and Jenny needed someone to give her a lift—her car's in for a service or something—so I said I'd go along."

I fitted the last sandwich into the tin, wedged in an apple and a bar of fruit-and-nut chocolate, and passed it over to him.

"There's a can of something in the larder—or do you want a flask of coffee?"

"A can'll be fine. Thanks, Ma. I don't know when I'll be back. See you."

Gathering up the sandwiches and the can, he was gone. As I began the task of clearing away the debris and sweeping up the crumbs from the floor, I smiled slightly to myself. If Michael was prepared to spend the day hanging about the moor on the off chance of spotting (or more likely not spotting) some bird, simply to be with Jenny, then perhaps he was more serious than I had imagined. Or maybe he was just being friendly and helpful. Either way, the fresh air would do him good.

When he returned that evening, rather damp but in good spirits, he seemed to have taken in more than the fresh air.

"It was super. We saw a hobby *and* a bittern. Have you ever seen a bittern? Most peculiar thing—very odd beak and makes an appalling noise."

"The bittern boometh," I said vaguely. "What does that come from?"

"Some poem," Michael said. "Anyway, it was pretty good. The sandwiches were fine," he added kindly. "Oh, yes," he added as he turned to go upstairs. "Poor old Ronnie Graham was there—he looked awful."

"Oh, yes, of course," I said. "He's a great bird-watcher, isn't he? How do you mean, awful?"

"Sort of gray and thin. He looked," Michael paused, looking for the right word, *"harassed."*

"I don't think he's properly over that flu," I said, "and he was very upset about his aunt's death—she was his only relative, after all. There's always a lot to do when someone dies anyway, and so much worse after a murder. I mean, he can't even arrange the funeral yet—not until the body's been released."

"I suppose so," Michael said doubtfully. "And being married to Carol can't be a picnic!"

As it happened, I heard from Ronnie the very next day.

"The funeral's on Friday," he said in that low, hesitant voice I always have difficulty in hearing properly on the phone. "At St. James's, two-thirty, and then the cemetery—she didn't want to be cremated. And there'll be a cup of tea here afterward, if you'd like to come."

I thanked him and said that I would be there.

There was a pause, and then he said, "I've been meaning to get in touch, to say how sorry I was—you finding her and everything—but I haven't been very well and it was such a shock . . ."

"Of course," I said. "I quite understand. It must have been a difficult time for you. And then there's all the clearing up to do and sorting out—it always takes ages."

"Yes," he agreed, "there's all that to be done. Actually Dr. Cowley's been very good—he said to take as long as we needed to clear the flat."

I gave a little snort of indignation.

"If he'd been as thoughtful to your aunt when she was alive," I said, "she'd have been spared a great deal of worry and upset in the last weeks of her life!"

*   *   *

THERE WEREN'T many people at the funeral. St. James's, which is an old and rather beautiful church, felt cold and empty, and our footsteps seemed to echo as we walked to our places. Apart from Ronnie and his wife, Carol, sitting at the front, there were a couple of elderly ladies who made their way down the aisle with some difficulty, one with a walking frame and the other with two sticks, friends of Miss Graham's from her youth, come to pay their respects to one more of their generation gone forever. Rosemary had come with me ("Jack's awfully sorry, but he's got this meeting in Bristol, and Mother has a bad cold"), and Michael was there as the representative of his firm. Roger was there, too, in his official capacity, and I recognized the reporter from the West *Somerset Gazette*—being murdered does, I suppose, mean that your funeral gets a mention in the local press.

I was glad that the vicar, who does tend to be rather consciously "modern," seemed quite subdued, and the words of the twenty-third Psalm, "the valley of the shadow of death" seemed, given the circumstances of Miss Graham's death, even more poignant than usual. It was as we were singing "The day thou gavest, Lord, is ended" and I was half turned, watching the coffin being carried back up the aisle, that I noticed Dr. Cowley sitting near the back of the church. Rosemary noticed, too, because she nudged me and whispered in my ear, "Can you believe it? The nerve of some people!"

But Dr. Cowley was not at the cemetery nor was he at Ronnie and Carol's house.

"You saw that awful man was at the church!" Rosemary said to Roger. "How he had the nerve!"

"He was her doctor, I suppose," Roger said.

"Yes, but when you think that he probably *murdered* her."

"We don't know that," Roger said firmly, putting down his teacup on a small and rather elegant Victorian table, "so really, Rosemary, you'd better not go around saying so!"

I'd never been inside the Grahams' house before, so I looked around with some interest. From the outside it was a perfectly ordinary semidetached house on the outskirts of Taviscombe, with a neat, unimaginatively laid-out garden and a view of the hills beyond the town. Inside, however, it was furnished with great good taste, with white walls and doors and plain curtains and carpets to show off the pieces of excellently proportioned furniture (mostly Victorian or Edwardian, though there were a few earlier pieces) and some fine prints in Hogarth frames. I don't know why I should have been surprised, but I was certainly impressed.

Carol came toward us, bearing a plate of sandwiches. We all dutifully took one, though I don't imagine anyone felt much like eating. She was dressed in a navy skirt and cardigan with a white blouse, the nearest most of us seem to get to mourning nowadays, and the dark clothes made her look washed out and tired. Her short, fairish hair was going gray, and she wore no makeup.

"It must be a very difficult time for you," I said, realizing that I was repeating my remark to Ronnie, but, quite honestly, what else is there to say at such a time?

"It's certainly been a nuisance not being able to arrange the funeral or move anything at the flat." Carol spoke sharply, in her usual rather abrupt manner. She looked doubtfully at Roger as if uncertain in what capacity he was there. "I know the police have to do their duty, but it's been very awkward, not knowing when we can get on and get things sorted. I haven't got a lot of time to do it—I have to spend all day in the shop and then there's all the bookkeeping . . . It hasn't helped, having Ronnie ill like this."

"No," I said, "he seems to have had a really bad go of this awful flu. I do hope you didn't catch it, too."

"Oh, I've no time to be ill," Carol replied brusquely. She looked tired and harassed, and, in spite of her ungracious reply, I felt sorry for her, knowing that it would be she who would have to do the clearing up and sorting out of Ronnie's aunt's belongings, and, though I knew she wouldn't be emotionally affected by the pathos of the final dispersal of Miss Graham's little world, she would have

the sheer hard work of it all. I recalled similar moments in my own life and remembered vividly the
aching back from bending over for hours sorting
out objects, wrapping china, and putting things into
cardboard boxes and suitcases, debating what
should be kept, what sent to the charity shop, clearing out the cupboards—the half-used packets of
corn flour, the never-opened tin of asparagus kept
for a special occasion.

"If there's anything I can do to help," I said, "do
please let me know."

Carol gave me a brief smile.

"Thanks," she said, "I expect I'll manage. But
thanks for offering."

There was a slightly constrained silence, and to
break it I said, "What a beautiful little cabinet you
have, that one on the sideboard, all that gorgeous
ormolu! Is it French?"

"Oh, you'll have to ask Ronnie," Carol said dismissively. "It's one of his things; he's mad about old
pieces. Dreadful things for catching the dust—he
has to look after them himself; I haven't time to
fiddle with them." She waved the plate of sandwiches in my direction and I took one meekly. "He's
picked them up at sales over the years, the furniture, too—he says they're an investment, but *he'll*
never sell them. Much better to put your money
into a building society, or back in the business; it
needs it, God knows. Oh, excuse me, Miss Gibbons
is leaving and I'd better give her a hand, else she'll

have something over with that walking frame! Ronnie! Miss Gibbons wants to go home—you said you'd drive her."

Ronnie, who had been talking to the vicar, came over to us.

"I'm so sorry, Sheila," he said. "I've got to take Miss Gibbons home—I did want to have a little chat about Aunt Mabel. Michael, Rosemary . . ." He acknowledged their presence with a little wave of his hand and moved over to Miss Gibbons. I had the feeling he'd been avoiding me, a feeling that was strengthened by the fact that when I turned to look after him, I found that he, too, had turned and was regarding me with a curiously nervous expression. Our eyes met and he looked away hastily, leaving me feeling puzzled and rather annoyed.

"Poor old Ronnie!" Rosemary said as we got into the car. "I know he's a bit wet, but honestly Carol is so—I don't know—so *difficult*. Aggressive almost, quite rude really, and dreadfully bossy."

"I suppose she's always had to be," I replied as I gave my seat belt a tug to free it. "Ronnie would have made a terrible failure of the shop if she hadn't taken him in hand. You remember how awful it was after old Mr. Graham died—I mean, it was a thriving little business in his day, but Ronnie let it get really run down, never anything in the size you wanted, or the color. Dreadful! It was only after he married Carol that things got back to normal again, and now I should think they do pretty well."

"Yes, I suppose so," Rosemary said grudgingly, "but she's lost several customers to my certain knowledge by that manner of hers."

"I always think that groveling about at people's feet, fitting shoes onto them, might bring out the revolutionary in the mildest person," I said reflectively, "not to mention having to trek back and forth to the stock room to bring out yet *another* pair of shoes that the customer won't buy anyway!"

"What always maddens me," Rosemary said, "is the way when you've *said* a size six B court shoe in navy they invariably bring you a six C black walking shoe or something equally irrelevant."

I slowed down to avoid a cat that suddenly darted across the road.

"I thought Ronnie looked pretty awful, didn't you?"

"Terribly *thin*—I don't suppose Carol feeds him properly," Rosemary replied. "And didn't you think it was a bit odd that he didn't speak to anyone except the vicar all the time we were there—didn't thank us for coming or anything. I mean, it's not that one *wants* to be thanked, but it is usual!"

"Yes, I noticed that. Still, I suppose the circumstances are a bit out of the ordinary—poor Miss Graham being murdered. I don't suppose any of us would know quite *how* we'd react if someone close to us died like that."

· 9 ·

The days went by, apparently busy and full of events, and yet, when one looked back, nothing much was accomplished. I was reviewing an American book on Mrs. Oliphant and was torn between admiration for the author's scholarship and research, and fury at the jargon-ridden writing in which she had presented it.

"It's no good," I said to Tris, who had taken up his customary position at my feet under the desk. "I really can't be doing with it anymore today!"

Recognizing a tone in my voice that indicated a cessation of work, Tris got up, shook himself, and barked several times, which brought Tessa into the room through the half-open door. She stood with her head tilted to one side, apparently considering the possibility of some sort of action on my part. I regarded the appealing spaniel eyes with some asperity and then said, "It's a miserable day, but all right, we'll go for a walk."

At the magic word *walk,* they both raced out into the hall, where I could hear Tris scratching impatiently at the front door.

The weather really was thoroughly depressing—gray, overcast, and cold with a biting wind and an imminent threat of rain—but I forced myself to get out of the car on the Promenade. I joined the dogs on the beach, where they were rushing about madly as though released from months of rigorous incarceration. Apparently I was the only person silly enough to venture out on such a day, because I had the beach entirely to myself, except for a few sea birds disconsolately pecking away at microscopic organisms at the water's edge. Looking up from the beach, I could see one or two people walking briskly along the Promenade, not pausing today to lean on the seawall and contemplate the gray-brown waters of the Bristol Channel, flecked here and there with dirty white foam whipped up by the wind.

The dogs seemed oblivious of the weather and ran, barking deliriously, in circles in and out of the rock pools while I, made miserable by the cold wind stinging my ears (I'd come out in such a hurry that I'd forgotten my hat and scarf), thought sourly of having to dry them and brush off the damp sand. I trudged along with my head down until I felt I'd had enough, and, calling the dogs, I turned to make my way back to where I'd left the car. They, however, were in the sort of mad mood that wind sometimes induces in animals and, seemingly deaf to my cries, raced away down the beach. Hurrying as best I could against the wind, I finally caught up with them and clipped on their leads, scolding them as I did so.

As I stood for a moment, getting back my breath, I was relieved to feel that the wind had abated a little, but, even as I noted this moderation, the first heavy drops of rain were falling; within seconds I was caught in a torrential downpour. Dragging the dogs behind me, I ran as quickly as I could along the beach, up the steps, and into one of the shelters on the Promenade, where I collapsed, extremely wet and breathless, onto the green painted seat carved with the initials of long-gone young vandals. The floor was unpleasantly littered with sodden scraps of paper, cigarette ends, and the odd bread crust, brought by some animal lover to feed the seagulls and blown in here, disregarded.

I sat there miserably, my wet hair dripping uncomfortably down my neck, with two very damp dogs shaking themselves over my legs, watching the rain streaming down the glass walls of the shelter. The rain outside was heavy, like a curtain pulled down between me and the sea, which was almost invisible.

I was just trying ineffectually to dry my hair with a couple of tissues I'd found in my pocket, when there was a sudden flurry and another person came into the shelter, trying to right a blown-inside-out umbrella. It was Dr. Cowley. For a moment he was too busy wrestling with his umbrella to notice there was another occupant of the shelter. Then, as he sat down gingerly on the seat, removed his glasses, and wiped the rain off them, he became aware of my presence.

"Ah," he said. "Good afternoon. What dreadful weather." Then, putting his glasses back on, he recognized me and continued, "Mrs. Malory, is it not?"

I had known Dr. Cowley for many years by sight and had, indeed, met him briefly on various social occasions. However, it was somehow disconcerting to be addressed by name—perhaps feeling that my wet and bedraggled appearance might have served in some way as a disguise.

"Yes," I said stiffly. "Good afternoon."

Dr. Cowley stood his dripping umbrella in a corner of the shelter and wiped his hands on a white handkerchief.

"I usually take a brief walk after lunch," he said, "when I am able to do so. I find it aids the digestion. But today, alas, I miscalculated the inclemency of the weather."

"It is very wet," I replied formally.

He looked at me inquiringly and then continued, "I am glad to have this opportunity of saying how distressed I am about the unhappy business of poor Miss Graham. It must have been most upsetting for you, finding her like that. And the shocking result of the postmortem!"

"That she was murdered, you mean?" I brought

out the word deliberately, and he looked away, as if by avoiding my eye he could disassociate himself from the brutal fact.

"Indeed," he said. "A terrible thing."

A sudden gust of wind rattled the glass panes of the shelter and blew a scurry of rain inside. Tessa moved over and cowered against Dr. Cowley's legs and he pushed the wet animal aside with an impatient exclamation. Irritated by this I suddenly found myself saying, "*You* were on West Hill just before she was killed, weren't you?"

He turned his head quickly and gave me a searching stare. "That is not so," he said sharply. "I was in Dulverton all morning."

Feeling that I had somehow burned my boats and had nothing to lose, I persisted. "Sybil Jacobs saw you, about eleven o'clock."

"She was mistaken," he replied.

I looked at him steadily.

"Sybil Jacobs isn't the sort of person who makes that kind of mistake. She said you nearly ran her over."

He didn't reply, and for a few moments we were both silent, listening to the sound of the storm outside. Tess moved over to me, and I stroked her wet head mechanically while Tris gave little whining noises indicative of discontent.

Dr. Cowley took out the white handkerchief again and wiped his face.

"I am aware," he said, "of the rumors that are

circulating in the town. It seems that there are certain people who think that I killed Miss Graham."

"No one else," I replied, "had a motive for wishing her dead. You wanted her out of Kimberley Lodge so that you could go ahead with your plans for a nursing home."

"That is true. But you must know that I did try to arrange alternative accommodation for her—"

"She wouldn't have taken it," I broke in. "She didn't *want* to move. You realized that. You knew you'd never get her out that way."

"And so you think I killed her?"

Tris whined again, and I gave a shiver, not entirely due to my cold and wet condition.

"It would have suited you to have her dead," I replied. "And if you were seen near Kimberley Lodge at just the time she was killed . . ."

"The police accept that I was in Dulverton." Dr. Cowley's voice was steely, and I had some difficulty keeping mine steady as I said, "No, I don't think they do. The patients you said you saw that morning were pretty vague. I think the police are keeping a fairly open mind."

"Ah, yes," Dr. Cowley said smoothly. "I had forgotten, you are personally acquainted with Chief Inspector Eliot, are you not? You are, perhaps, in his confidence in this matter?"

"No, of course Roger doesn't discuss police business with me," I said quickly. "But he has asked for my help on several occasions—since I knew Miss

Graham well, and, of course, finding the body and everything."

"I see."

He seemed to be debating something in his mind, and his hand holding the handkerchief clenched and unclenched upon it. Finally he gave a sigh and said, "I think I must tell you something. Whether you choose to pass it on to the police is up to you."

He looked at me and I nodded assent.

"Very well. First of all, I must admit that I was indeed in the area of West Hill at the time you have mentioned, but I swear to you that my presence there had nothing whatever to do with Miss Graham's death."

I sat very still, anxious that no movement on my part should disturb his narrative.

"Some years ago," he went on, "I had an assistant, a nurse attached to my practice. Her name was June Hargreaves. Our relationship was, in fact, not simply professional, if you understand my meaning."

He paused and I murmured something that might be taken as comprehension.

"One of my patients," he continued, "an old lady, died and left me quite a considerable sum of money. She had no relatives, and toward the end of her life she had come to rely upon me, not simply as a doctor but as a friend. One of the things she consulted me about was her will. She hadn't made one and was concerned about what she should do. Of course, I said that she should see her solicitor, but

she was unwilling to do so, having a dislike of anything to do with the legal profession—apparently
her father had had some unfortunate experience . . .
So I drew up for her a simple form of a will, and
Nurse Hargreaves and her daily woman both wit-
nessed it."

I shifted slightly on the uncomfortable wooden
seat.

"I see."

"It was perfectly legal," Dr. Cowley said quickly
"and was passed for probate with no problems."

"But?" I inquired.

"But when the will had been proved and she realized the extent of the legacy, Nurse Hargreaves im-
plied that I had used undue influence to persuade
a patient to make me her legatee. Unfortunately,
she—Nurse Hargreaves, that is—had misunderstood
our relationship. She had some idea of marriage—
absolutely out of the question. Although I was a
widower, it would have been quite unsuitable, and
when I told her that marriage was impossible, she
threatened to make a scandal—the papers, the
BMA, everyone."

"But if you'd done nothing wrong," I said suspi-
ciously, "why should you have been worried?"

I could imagine only too well. Dr. Cowley's oleaginous approach to his elderly patient, the old-world
charm and courtesy, the attentive visits—influence,
certainly, whether or not it might be called undue—

nothing criminal exactly, but not within the ethics of his profession.

"And of course," I said, remembering Mrs. Dudley's disapprobation, "there was the business of old Miss Benson—all that would have been brought up again."

He started slightly at Miss Benson's name and said bitterly, "I cannot think why I ever came back to this town, where all people ever do is indulge in unfounded gossip. I should have stayed in Rome after my wife died, except . . ."

He broke off, and I remembered hearing that there had also been gossip about his wife's death and the large sum of money she had left him.

"People have long memories," I said, "and not only in Taviscombe."

He appeared disconcerted by my remark and, for a moment, made no reply. Then he went on. "I gave Nurse Hargreaves a sum of money—quite a large amount—on the condition that she went abroad. She emigrated to Australia, Queensland, I believe, and married out there. However," he said and sighed, "that was not the end of it. I suppose I was foolish to believe that it could be. A short while ago, I heard from her. She was now a widow and had returned to England. She wanted to see me; she was very insistent about that."

"I see."

"She was staying in one of those small hotels on West Hill and insisted that I should visit her at eleven o'clock on that Monday morning—the day Miss Graham was killed. I explained that that was my day for going to Dulverton and that I would see her some other time, but she seemed to think that I was *fobbing her off*, as she put it, and became quite hysterical. Since she was apparently using a public telephone in the hall of the hotel, I simply couldn't take the risk of letting her go on—someone might have heard her—so I agreed to see her then."

Tris was moving restlessly (Tessa had gone resignedly to sleep by my feet), and I put a hand on his head to quieten him. I didn't want to miss any of this.

"It was awkward—I had to rearrange things at Dulverton, though fortunately there were only house visits to be done; no one in the surgery. Anyway, I picked her up at her hotel, and we drove over to West Hill, out along the old military road, where I hoped no one would see us. I tried to reason with her, but, in the end, I was obliged to part with a large sum of money to keep her quiet, and she promised to go back to Leamington, which is apparently where she was now living with her sister."

He broke off and, removing his glasses again, rubbed his eyes. He looked weary and under strain—an old man, and, just for a moment, I couldn't help feeling sorry for him. Then I remembered Miss Graham and how he had harassed her— if nothing worse. But *had* there been anything worse? I was uncertain now.

As if scenting my uncertainty, he said abruptly, "Do you believe me? That is where I was on the morning that Miss Graham was killed. You see how I couldn't tell the police what I had been doing—I couldn't risk it all coming out, even after all this time."

I hesitated, reluctant to let go of what seemed to be the only suspect in this sad case.

"Do you have that address in Leamington?" I asked.

"Yes."

"Well then, she, this Nurse Hargreaves, will be able to give you an alibi, won't she?"

He shrugged hopelessly.

"I don't know. I can hardly expect her to admit that she was blackmailing me, can I? The police may not believe me. Do you?"

He put the question to me suddenly, and I was taken off balance. It is always difficult to admit that someone you dislike, someone really unpleasant, unscrupulous, an opportunist—thoroughly *vile,* as my friend Linda would say—that someone like that could, perhaps, on this particular occasion, be telling the truth.

"Yes," I said reluctantly. "Yes, I think I do."

· 10 ·

Strangely enough, when I telephoned Roger that evening, he seemed to believe Dr. Cowley's story, too.

"Well," he said, "it would certainly explain why he felt the need to lie about his movements that morning. It's certainly not a thing he'd want to get about. I wonder," Roger went on thoughtfully, "why he told *you*, out of the blue, as it were?"

"I think it was the weather, really," I said. "It was such a dreadful day and there we both were so wet and miserable—you know how you feel at your lowest *ebb* at times like that—and then I suddenly faced him with having been seen by Sybil Jacobs . . . I was rather fierce with him, I suppose, and he just came out with it."

"Well, whatever," Roger said. "It's certainly worth pursuing. I'll get that address in Leamington from him and go down and see this June Hargreaves. If

I suddenly appear on her doorstep and ask her about seeing him that day she might just tell me the truth."

"She sounds pretty vindictive," I said, "from what Dr. Cowley said—a woman scorned and all that."

"Oh, well, even if she does deny all knowledge, if I see her face-to-face I can probably tell if she's lying."

Whether it was the result of getting so wet and sitting in that shelter in damp clothes I don't know, but I woke the following morning with a beastly sore throat that by the next day was a roaring cold, a streaming, sneezing, feverish horror. I dragged myself out of bed and tottered downstairs, but by the time I'd let the dogs out and given Foss a saucer of tinned food (rejected), I was obliged to collapse onto a kitchen chair, unable to contemplate any thought of breakfast.

"Ma, what on earth are you doing down here?" Michael said, coming in with the daily paper. "You look ghastly. Go right back to bed and I'll bring something up to you."

"I'm all right," I replied croakily. "You'll make yourself late for work. Anyway, what about your breakfast?" I said as Michael shooed me upstairs. "And can you feed the dogs when they come in and perhaps you could cut up a bit of that cooked rabbit for Foss; he doesn't like tinned stuff . . ."

I flopped back into bed, and after a while Michael brought up a cup of coffee and a piece of toast.

"Yes, I know you don't want anything to eat, but you shouldn't take aspirin on an empty stomach. Here. Sorry the coffee's slopped into the saucer— it's coming up the stairs that does it. Can you sit up? Mind the coffee doesn't drip onto the duvet. Yes, I've fed the animals and cooked my breakfast— bacon and fried egg, very nourishing. Right, now lie back and enjoy being an invalid. I'll come home at lunchtime and see how you're getting on. Bye."

Resolutely trying not to think of the chaos Michael had probably created in the kitchen, I lay back on my pillow and drifted off to sleep.

I was awoken by Foss landing heavily on my chest. Animals, of course, love people being ill in bed, helpless and entirely at their mercy. A large, loving Siamese face peered into mine, assessed the situation, and then settled down happily on the pillow beside me in such a way that I couldn't turn my head without getting fur in my face, and began his usual raucous purring. I suppose it must have lulled me to sleep, because when I awoke again it was lunchtime and Michael was standing beside the bed waving a tin of soup in either hand.

"Scotch broth or pea and ham? And don't say you don't want anything, because you always used to tell me that you had to feed a cold."

"Oh, pea and ham, please," I said weakly. "I don't think I can cope with all the *bits* in Scotch broth. What are you having? There's a pizza in the freezer, or one of those things you can heat up in the microwave . . ."

But Michael had gone. Foss, realizing that there was now a source of food downstairs, followed him. After a while, Michael reappeared with the soup and some toast cut neatly into triangles.

"I've poured you a glass of orange juice because of the vitamin C."

He set the tray down. "And, yes, it's all right— I've got a pizza in the oven. Now then, I'll nip into the market on my way back and get you a bit of fish for this evening—suitable invalid diet. *And*, if you're good and feeling better, I've got a most *peculiar* story to tell you. No, not a hint now. Eat up your soup, and all will be revealed this evening!"

I DIDN'T PAY much attention to Michael's promise of a strange story, thinking it was merely a ploy to cheer me up, but when he had cleared away the supper things ("Yes, I brought in some fish-and-chips for me, and *yes*, I've done all the washing up— this morning's as well") he sat down in a chair beside my bed with a cup of coffee and said, "Well, now. Are you sitting comfortably? Then I'll begin."

He put down the coffee cup.

"Many years ago, O best beloved, there was a cantankerous old farmer who lived over the other side of Taunton. His wife had died, he didn't have any children, and he couldn't stand any of his relatives, so he was rather stuck for someone to leave his farm to. Not that there was anything spectacular to leave; just a dilapidated farmhouse and about twenty acres of scruff, gorse, and rabbits. The only person he could stand the sight of for more than five minutes was his wife's niece, but being, as I said, a miserable old so-and-so, he couldn't quite bring himself to leave it to her outright, so in the end he made a will leaving her the life interest."

I straightened a slipping pillow and tried to take an intelligent interest, though my head felt as if it were stuffed full of cotton wool. "What's a life interest?"

"It means that she got the income the land produced, grass keep, and so on, for as long as she lived, but she couldn't sell the land and take the capital because there was a sitting tenant. And even if she had been able to sell, the proceeds would have to be invested and all she'd get would be the mingy bit of interest. As I said, it wasn't a case of his liking her the most of all his relatives so much as hating her the least."

"Goodness," I said, "real Cold Comfort Farm stuff!"

"That was the best the farmer could think of," Michael continued, "or, rather, his solicitor—an old-fashioned type who really loved the sort of will that would set a family at one another's throats. They must have had a jolly time working it out together! But it left the question of who was to have the land when his wife's niece died. In the end they both decided that *she'd* make the decision who'd inherit the capital when she popped off. We call that a power of appointment, by the way, though I don't suppose for one minute that you're interested."

I made a sound indicative of interest, and Michael went on. "Well, he died, but not before he'd lived in the house on his own for so long without spending any money on it that the only thing keeping it from falling down was force of habit. As for the land, the sitting tenant was equally ramshackle, only paying half a groat a year or something equally traditional, and the whole thing was more trouble than it was worth.

"Well, the niece forgot all about it, the house sort of slowly subsided, the rent on the land was paid to the solicitor, who used it to pay the rates and his fees, and that was that. I mean, why bother? In another seventy million years, the earth will probably collide with the sun, and nobody will either know or care."

I reached over and took a sip of orange juice to help me concentrate.

"So then what?"

"Ah," Michael said, "here the plot thickens ever so slightly, because, after about ten years, the sitting tenant went bankrupt, which ends the tenancy, and—and here it gets really exciting—when the latest area plan came out last year (that's the Planning Office's statement of policy for the next five years

or so, in case you wondered), the report made it
fairly obvious that for the first time it ought to be
possible to get planning permission on those twenty
acres, which means they're suddenly very valuable
indeed. In fact, one property developer has already
expressed an interest in building an estate of execu-
tive homes (whatever they may be) on the site."

"That's a nice stroke of luck for the wife's niece,"
I said, trying to keep a grasp of the narrative.

Michael grinned. "Would have been," he replied.
"The land would have been sold, the proceeds invested in stocks and shares, and she'd have had the
income off several million quid to see her through
her declining years. As it turned out, though, she
missed the boat."

"How?" I asked.

"She's dead. The wife's niece was old Miss Graham. Isn't that just," Michael opined, "like life?"

For a moment I couldn't take in the implications.

"You mean," I said slowly, "if all this had happened a bit earlier, she would have had that enormous amount of money—she wouldn't have had all
that hassle over the flat?"

"She could have bought up a fair slice of West
Hill."

"Oh *no*," I cried. "How awful! How unfair!"

Michael shrugged. "Whoever said life was fair?"
he said.

I blew my nose vigorously, as if by that I could

clear my head and try to understand the significance of Michael's amazing story.

"I suppose that means that Ronnie stands to inherit a great deal of money?"

"Ah, well, I'm not certain. It's a point of law I'm not sure about. I *think*, from what I could find out, that the old dear never used the power of appointment—you remember, the right to say who was to have the loot after she was gone—she'd have had to sign a deed, you see, actually naming someone. And I can't find anything in the files to say that she ever did so. No point, as far as she was concerned. Couldn't be bothered."

"I think I follow. So what will happen to the land? And the money?"

Michael shrugged again. "At the moment it's as clear as mud. You see, as far as I can make out, since nobody's named in the old man's will apart from old Miss Graham, and if she never used the power of appointment, then the whole caboodle may go to the Crown. Which will probably," Michael added, "fritter the whole lot away on urban renewal and infrastructure and stuff like that. Makes you sick really, doesn't it?"

"It certainly seems jolly unfair," I said. "Especially to poor Miss Graham."

I finished off the orange juice. "Are you sure?"

"Well, no, I'm not," he said. "Since I am but a humble articled clerk and not up in the finer points of the whatsit. I was going to ask Edward, but he's in Bristol today and Philip was busy with the painters all day. It's maddening that today's Friday, so we'll have to wait until Monday before I can continue with my inquiries, as it were."

"It's an extraordinary story," I said. "Do you suppose it gives anyone a motive for killing Miss Graham? I can't help feeling that a couple of million pounds has to be a motive for *someone*."

"I suppose it might be the Treasury, panting to get its hands on the dosh," Michael said, "but I think you might have a job proving it."

I laughed. "No little gray men in bowlers with briefcases hanging around West Hill? Oh, dear, we shouldn't laugh. It's awful really."

"Well," Michael said, gathering up my glass and his coffee cup, "I thought it might divert your thoughts from your invalidish state. Shall I switch on your telly for the news?"

I DON'T KNOW if it was the effect of Michael's amazing story or what, but I felt very much better the next day and by Monday morning I was more or less back to normal again. Certainly well enough to do my usual shopping trip to the supermarket. It really is extraordinary how, if you turn your back on the housekeeping for even a couple of days, you mysteriously find you've run out of practically all the basics. ("But, Michael, you can't have used a whole pack of dishwasher powder?") and have to start again from scratch.

I was just trying to decide whether or not the "10 percent extra FREE" justified my choosing a different brand of coffee from my usual one, when Rosemary came round the corner of the beverages shelves. She was attempting to push a trolley with one hand, while trying with the other to retain some control over a small child who was making a determined bid for freedom.

"Oh, thank goodness. Sheila. Could you take this wretched trolley for a minute while I get Delia—she insisted on walking round with me, but she's in one of her wild moods." She scooped her granddaughter up and dumped her unceremoniously in the child seat of the trolley. "Now *do* be a good girl and sit there nicely while Grandma does the shopping."

Delia opened her mouth to howl, thought better of it, and fixed me with that unwinking stare young children often employ and which I find so unnerving.

"Hello, Delia," I said. "Do you remember me?"

She gave no sign of recognition but continued to regard me fixedly.

"Where doggies?" she asked suddenly.

"Doggies at home," I said.

"*Why* doggies at home?"

"Doggies not like shopping," I replied, feeling like a Portuguese language course.

Delia appeared to lose interest in me and the whereabouts of the dogs and devoted her attention to a packet of chocolate buttons that Rosemary had deviously introduced into her hand.

"You seem to have your hands full," I said.

"Well," Rosemary said, leaning wearily on the handles of the trolley, "it's Jilly's day for taking the baby to the clinic, so I thought it would be easier if I had Delia. Unfortunately," she continued, "Delia managed to break one of Mother's ornaments while we were round there—so ridiculous leaving all those breakable things at child level and then complaining that Jilly never takes the children to see her!—so I'm feeling more than usually harassed. How about you? You look a bit fragile."

"Oh, I'm all right—just getting over a rotten cold. I'd better not breathe too near you or Delia in case I'm still infectious."

"Oh, Taviscombe is full of germs at the moment," Rosemary said. "I daren't go into the chemist! Talking of which, I saw Ronnie Graham on Friday and he still looks awful. If I were Carol, I'd be really worried about him. It can't *still* be the aftereffect of flu after all this time."

"He always was a rather sickly child," I said. "Miss Graham used to worry about him."

"Oh, well, perhaps this marketing course he's going on this week will buck him up—it's in Birmingham, I think he said, which isn't exactly . . . Still, it'll be a change of scene for him."

"Oh, by the way," I said, "talking of Miss Graham

and Ronnie, Michael told me the most amazing thing—"

I was interrupted by Delia, who, having now finished all the chocolate buttons, decided that she was going to protest after all. She let out a tremendous wail. Rosemary gave me a look and said, "Sorry, I'd better go. She's capable of keeping this up for hours! What is it they say about the terrible twos? I'm sure Jilly wasn't as difficult when she was that age. Maybe it's just that I'm older!"

She moved quickly toward the checkout, and I continued with my shopping.

By the time I'd finished, there were long queues at all the checkouts. Choosing one that seemed to have the least number of ladened trolleys, I found myself (as I so often do) landed at the checkout with the faulty till, and, since I'd already loaded all my purchases onto the conveyor belt thing, I was trapped there until it was seen to by the supervisor.

"Isn't it maddening!" a voice behind me said. "This always seems to happen to me!"

I turned and found Jenny Drummond standing behind me. She was looking particularly handsome in a green-gray coat that set off the color of her magnificent hair that today she was wearing swept up in a coil on top of her head.

"Oh, hello, Jenny. Yes, it's always the same—banks, post offices, supermarkets—I always manage to pick the dud one!"

She smiled. "I wouldn't mind, only it's my lunch

break and I'm a bit rushed. How are you? Michael said you'd had a bad cold."

"Oh, I'm all right now. Michael did his ministering angel bit over the weekend, so I was able to stay in bed for a day. I always think it clears up quicker if you can."

"Is Michael a good cook?" Jenny asked.

"We-ell, much as I'd like to give him a glowing reference. I'm afraid he's a rather limited one—beans on toast or a good fry-up. But he did manage a bit of smoked haddock for me, bless his heart."

Jenny laughed.

"Talking of food," I went on, "do come and have supper with us one evening."

"Oh, that *would* be nice. I'd love to."

"Can we fix a day?"

"Well, it'll have to be next week, I'm afraid—I'm off tomorrow to spend a few days with my aunt who lives near Worcester."

"That sounds nice. It's a very pleasant part of the country. Do you visit her often?"

Jenny pulled a wry face. "Not as often as I should, I'm afraid. She's a good soul and my only surviving relative, but—how can I put it?—we don't have much in common. Her life is very much bound up with the church in the village and good works and things like that. Not wildly exciting!"

"Oh, well," I said soothingly. "You'll probably have a good rest, and I'm sure it will do you good."

She laughed. "I don't know that a *rest* is really

what I want. Life, at the moment, seems so very *unexciting*, uninspired—boring, I suppose."

"But I'm sure you've managed to make lots of friends in Taviscombe," I said. "A lively girl like you!"

"Oh, well, there are a few people at badminton, and with the ornithologists and at work—but they're really just acquaintances, not proper friends."

"There's Michael," I suggested.

She gave me a quick look. "Oh, yes, there's Michael, and he's really been so very nice and such good company . . ." Her voice died away and I was left uncertain as to what exactly she did think of Michael, which, I suppose, was her intention. A clever girl, Jenny.

"Anyway," she went on, "I'll look forward very much to coming to supper when I get back—I still remember that delicious lemon tart. Would you be very kind and let me have the recipe? I love cooking; it's so relaxing when you've had a hard day at work or feel all tensed up over something. Oh, hooray! They've fixed the till at last. Now maybe we can get a move on!"

As I wheeled my trolley out into the car park, I wondered about Jenny. A strangely self-contained girl, lively, charming even, but it was difficult to know what she was thinking, what sort of person she really was. *Aloof* was the word that came to mind. Perhaps when she came to supper again, I'd be able to get to know her better.

· II ·

"**W**ell!" Michael said, coming in and throwing his coat in the general direction of the hall chest. "There's a turnup for the book!"

"What is?" I asked, retrieving the coat and going to hang it up. "Oh, dear, this loop's gone *again*! I don't know what you do with your things!"

"Oh, do leave it! It's really a most amazing thing." He followed me into the kitchen. "Old Miss Graham and that business of the power of appointment. I asked Edward about it today."

"What about it?"

"*Well.* You know that a lot of the standard clauses in wills are bunged in automatically now on the word processor, and you just fill in the personal bits. Well, there's this particular clause that says"— Michael took a deep breath and intoned with relish— " 'I give all my real and personal property whatsoever and wheresoever not hereby or by any codicil hereto otherwise specifically disposed of (including any property over which I may have a general power of appointment or disposition by will) to . . .' It's smashing stuff, isn't it? Anyway, there you are."

"You mean . . ."

"I mean that validly, if unintentionally, she's passed the trust fund on to Ronnie, along with the little bit of money she had in her own right."

"Goodness," I said.

"Furthermore," Michael said, "you remember the property developer I told you about? Well, it appears that he's surfaced again; made a definite offer. The Taunton solicitor—the one who drew up the old man's will—has written to Edward about it."

"What an extraordinary coincidence."

"Isn't it just!"

"So," I said thoughtfully, "Ronnie's going to be a very rich man indeed."

"So he is."

We were both silent for a moment considering the implications of this.

Then Michael said, "It's a terrific motive."

"Absolutely," I agreed. "Roger says he always likes there to be a money motive in any case he's dealing with. I wonder," I added, "if Edward has told him about all this?"

"Client confidentiality," Michael said. "By rights I shouldn't have told *you* anything about it."

"No, I suppose not. Still, it *is* a murder investigation."

"Anyway," Michael said, "Ronnie's such a *wimp*. I mean, you couldn't imagine him doing anyone in!"

"No," I said, "and there's the business of the poison in the cakes. I mean, they were homemade, and *he* couldn't have made them."

"But Carol could have. She's a much better suspect. Anyway, poison's a woman's crime."

"I've got a feeling," I said, "that that's a sexist remark and no longer a politically correct theory."

"No, but seriously, Ma, it's much more likely."

"But could they have known about this power of appointment thing, though?" I asked.

"As far as I know, no one at the firm has said anything. Law firms being as they are, and with things moving at the speed of a geriatric glacier—as you well know—we haven't really done anything about old Miss G's probate yet, and I've only just started to delve about into the file."

I began grating the cheese for the Bolognaise.

"I suppose," I said, "Miss Graham *might* have mentioned it—in general terms—and they somehow cottoned onto it."

"It's possible, I suppose, though I don't get the impression she'd really grasped what it was all about."

"No, she hated any sort of forms or legal things, I know, and she was always a bit vague and unbusinesslike—that's why the wool shop packed up."

"Too woolly minded to cope," Michael said and grinned. "Sorry. No, as I say, Ronnie's much too wet to have worked out anything like that, but Carol's pretty sharp, and if there was money involved she'd be onto it like a ferret down a drain."

"Well, they both have a motive," I said, "but are we suspicious of Carol because we're rather sorry for Ronnie and don't particularly like her?"

"Likes and dislikes don't really come into it." Michael began picking at bits of cheese as they came out of the grater. "She's much more capable of murder than he is—a right little Lady Macbeth, I'd say."

" 'Give *me* the daggers!' Yes, I could hear her saying that all right—here let *me* do it! If you think about it, Macbeth must have been quite a difficult person to live with—all that inviting guests home without checking first."

"*Yes*, Ma. But about Carol. Where was she when old Miss Graham was killed?"

"Let me see. I rang up the girl in the shop to try and get Ronnie, and *he* was at home in bed with flu and Carol—Carol had gone to Taunton to see a supplier. I wonder?"

"What are you going to do, Ma? Ask Roger if he's checked her alibi?"

"No. I think I'll just ask a few questions myself . . . Oh bother, I've grated my finger. Pass me an Elastoplast from the cupboard, will you?"

THE NEXT DAY, I waited until I saw Carol leave the shop for her lunch (she took it at two o'clock when what passes for the lunchtime rush hour in Taviscombe was over) and the young assistant was alone. What Ronnie was doing I couldn't imagine. He seemed to be spending less and less time in the business.

"Oh, good afternoon," I said brightly. "I want a pair of walking shoes in brown, low heels, size six and a half, C fitting."

The girl disappeared for a while and finally came back with a motley selection of shoes, some of which were neither brown nor low-heeled, but since that was not the object of the exercise, I didn't comment but let her help me try them on.

"No, that's a bit tight on the instep . . . No, this one's a bit better . . . Is Mrs. Graham about?"

"No." The girl produced a shoehorn and tried her best to cram my foot into a shoe that was manifestly too tight. "She's on her lunch break. Did you want to see her specially?"

"No, no. I just wondered how she and Mr. Graham are after that terrible business with his aunt."

The girl gave up her struggle with the shoe.

"I think you really need a wider fitting in this style," she said. "Yes, wasn't it awful? Poisoned, the papers said. Fancy having someone close to you *poisoned*."

"Yes, indeed," I said. "It was most distressing. Actually," I lowered my voice confidentially, "I was the one who found her."

The girl sat back on her heels and regarded me

with round eyes, as if I was some sort of television celebrity.

"Really!" she said. "You found her! Then you must be the lady who phoned me that day asking for Mr. Graham!"

"That's right," I replied. "I'm Mrs. Malory, and I was a friend of poor Miss Graham." I looked at her inquiringly. "And your name is?"

"Julie—Julie Shallcross."

"Oh, really. I think I know your mother—Maureen Shallcross?—at the Hospital Friends. Well, Julie, as you can imagine, I was dreadfully upset and, of course, I needed to get hold of one of them right away."

Julie nodded solemnly and regarded me with frank curiosity. I was obviously beginning to take on for her the glamour of someone in a newspaper story. "It must have been awful, all alone like that with a dead person. I've never seen anyone dead."

"It was certainly awkward, neither of them being available," I said. "Mrs. Graham was in Taunton, I think you said?"

"Yes, she went to see Mr. Bracewell—he's our handbag supplier. He's on that trading estate near Staplegrove."

"And she was out all day then?"

Julie settled herself more comfortably on a small fitting stool, obviously prepared to embark on a good chat.

"Yes, she was. Though as it turned out the whole thing was a waste of time."

"Really," I said. "Why was that?"

"He wasn't there. He'd been called away—urgent family business, he said. He'd had to go away the night before, so there was no one there. He works on his own, you see. *She* wasn't half cross when she got back."

Julie's face darkened at the memory. "She thought he hadn't let her know. Apparently he'd left a message on their answering machine, but it turns out it wasn't working properly—I expect *Mr.* Graham had done something to it (he's not very good with mechanical things)—and she never got it."

"How tiresome for her," I said sympathetically. "But you say she was out all day?"

"Oh, well, as she said, since she was in Taunton anyway there were several other things she had to see to, shopping and so on."

"Oh, yes," I replied. "There are so many things you simply can't get in Taviscombe anymore, and you really *have* to go to Taunton for them."

"Taviscombe's a bit of a dead place really, not much to do."

Julie balanced a shoe reflectively in her hand. "No proper disco and nowhere for any decent group to come."

"No," I said, "I suppose it must seem a bit slow for you. I don't remember really, it's so long since I was your age. But I seem to think that we made our own entertainment more. We had to get about on bicycles, too—it wasn't long after the war, and hardly anyone had cars and no petrol to speak of, so we couldn't go far . . ."

Julie looked at me as if I were from a different planet rather than simply a different age, so I said briskly, "I quite like this one with the buckle, if you have it in a larger size."

Julie shook her head.

"We could order it for you," she suggested.

"Oh, well, I'll leave it then." I picked up my handbag. "I'll look in again and see if you've got anything new. Thank you so much, Julie. Do remember me to your mother."

I felt rather mean, leaving the poor girl to put away the rejected shoes that I had had no intention of buying, but I consoled myself by thinking that she must be used to it by now, and she had at least had a chat to pass what would otherwise have been a boring gap in her day.

"I THINK you should tell Roger," Michael said when I reported back to him that evening. "It means that Carol doesn't have an alibi and she *does* have a zonking great motive. It sounds a bit thin, all that about the answer-phone being up the pictures."

"Yes," I said thoughtfully. "Goodness, I've just realized! When I tried to phone Ronnie at home, you know, when I found Miss Graham, there was no answer-phone—I mean, it just kept ringing through!"

"Ha! There you are. It must have been switched off by then, because if there'd been anything wrong with it you'd probably have got peculiar buzzing and clicking noises. It wouldn't have just rung through."

"So," I broke in, "this Bracewell, the handbag man, could perfectly well have left a message on the machine the night before, so she'd have known he wouldn't be there and *then* she pretended that the machine hadn't been working—probably just switched it off—in case anyone else tried to get through. And she didn't go to Taunton at all. And that business about spending the day shopping! If I know Carol and it had been as she said, she'd have been straight back to Taviscombe to the shop. Especially if Ronnie was ill and she'd had to leave Julie in charge—she's a nice girl, but, as I can testify, she's not much use at selling shoes! So Carol might have been in Taviscombe all the time. If only someone had seen *her* on West Hill!"

"Well, you can't expect that sort of luck twice," Michael said and laughed. "There's only one Sybil Jacobs!"

"Alas! Anyway, you're right. I'd better tell Roger." I got up reluctantly from the sofa and replaced a sleeping Foss carefully on the seat. "I think I'll call him at home, sort of casually, because, as you say, I really ought not to have known about that trust and all those legal things, and if I make it all official at the police station, you might get into trouble with Edward."

Roger was noncommittal when I told him what I'd found out.

"Yes. The power of appointment, we know about that. I'm looking into it."

My description of Carol's abortive trip to Taunton and the nonfunctioning answer-phone roused him a little though.

"*Did* she now! That's interesting—I'll follow it up. We can do with another lead because Dr. Cowley's definitely a non-starter."

"What?"

"I went to Leamington and, by dint of *not* implying any sort of blackmail, found out from this June Hargreaves that she *had* been with Cowley at about the time of the murder."

"Ah. It's a pity, though," I said and sighed. "He's such a thoroughly dislikable man; he'd have been a good murderer."

Roger laughed. "Life isn't like that, as well you know. Anyway, thank you, Sheila, for your help—oh, hang on, Rosemary wants a word. Something about gingerbread for the bonfire night party. I'll be in touch."

· 12 ·

"**A**re you going to the bonfire party?" I asked Jenny when she came to supper the following week.

"Michael's been telling me about it," she replied enthusiastically. "It sounds like great fun—I adore fireworks. We never had any when I was a child, and I've always felt deprived."

"Oh, dear. Did your parents disapprove of them?"

"My father died when I was a baby, so we were very poor and my mother used to say she hadn't got money to burn." Jenny gave a little laugh. "So we never did."

There was a moment's slightly embarrassed silence, and then I said quickly, "I'm a bit afraid of fireworks myself—I don't like the noise. And, of course, the animals hate it all. At least the dogs do. Foss seems impervious; in fact he usually sits by the window drinking it all in! Actually, this is a very well organized show, run by the Round Table in aid of charity, so we all chip in—contributing fireworks, food for the barbecue, and so on. Which reminds me, I *must* get the gingerbread made sometime this week!"

"How nice! Can I make something, too?" Jenny asked. "A cake or some biscuits—Oh, I know! I've got a very good recipe for brownies from an American cookbook. Would that do?"

"That would be lovely," I replied. "But you must be sure to keep them away from Michael, who's been known to eat six at a sitting!"

"Oh, it's very rewarding to have someone who really enjoys what you cook—just cooking for oneself isn't the same thing at all."

"Did your mother teach you to cook?" I asked.

Jenny shook her head. "No, she didn't like cooking—anyway, she was out at work all day and always pretty exhausted when she got in. No, I just sort of picked it up. And then, at the end, she was ill for a long time so . . ." Her voice trailed away.

"I'm so sorry," I said. "It must have been very hard for you."

Jenny gave a little grimace. "The hardest thing of all was not going to university—I had a place—but by then my mother was too ill for me to go away. Even Birmingham was too far—I had to be able to get home to see to her at lunchtime."

"Oh, my dear!"

Jenny smiled. "Oh, it wasn't the end of the world.

Lots of people have worse things to cope with. And I was lucky—I got this job in a solicitor's office in Wolverhampton, and they were very good—sent me on day release courses at the polytechnic for word processing and computer studies."

"What made you come to Taviscombe?" I asked.

"I saw the job advertised, and it was quite a step up for me, very good experience."

"Well," I said, "I do hope you stay here and we don't lose you to London and the big time!"

"She can't possibly go," Michael said. "Greene, Drayton, and Decker would simply collapse in a heap without her. Besides, she's the only person in the entire firm who can find anything in the document room."

Jenny smiled at him. "Oh, I like Taviscombe, and the countryside's so lovely round here."

"Of course," I said. "You're a bird-watcher, aren't you?"

"Well, in a very amateur way—I don't know an awful lot about them, but it's a good excuse for being in the open air in pleasant places."

I laughed and went out to get the coffee. When I got back Foss followed me into the room and made straight for Jenny, jumping onto her lap. She gave a little cry and I went over and scooped him up.

"I'm so sorry," I said apologetically, putting him on my chair, where he promptly curled up, wrapped his tail around his nose, and feigned sleep. "I'm afraid he does rather tend to land with his claws out; it can be very painful at times. I do hope he hasn't laddered your tights or pulled a thread in your skirt?"

"No, honestly," she said, picking the cat hairs off her skirt, "it's fine! Just that I wasn't expecting it."

"Oh, really, Ma," Michael said. "The animals get worse and worse! I swear Foss does it deliberately. It's a miracle anyone ever comes to see us!"

"I'm afraid you're right," I said. "He does have a dreadfully calculating nature. Did you have any animals at home?" I asked Jenny as I poured the coffee. "White for you, isn't it?"

"Yes, that's lovely, thanks. No, we never had animals—it wasn't really convenient with us both out all day."

"Yes, of course." I handed her the cup.

"What a lovely coffee set!" Jenny said, turning the cup round in its saucer to look at the pattern. "Royal Worcester, isn't it?"

"Yes, it is," I replied. "How clever of you to know—it's not one of the better-known designs."

"Oh, I love beautiful china and porcelain," she said. "If I had a lot of money, that's what I'd collect."

"This set belonged to my grandmother. There's a tea set as well, *almost* complete, though Foss knocked one of the cups off the draining board and broke it. I had it riveted, but of course it's not the same."

"Oh, dear, what a shame. I should think a complete set would be very valuable now."

"Probably," I replied. "I've never actually got around to finding out, I'm afraid. I suppose I should keep it put away in a cabinet, but I'm sure my grandmother would rather I used it; she was a very *practical* woman. Anyway, I can't bear to think of beautiful things locked away—jewelry in banks, pictures in strong rooms, that sort of thing. Did you see that bit in the paper the other day about how someone keeps a Stradivarius in a bank vault!"

"Well, it must be worth a fortune! They'd want to keep it safe."

"But an instrument like that!" I persisted. "If it's not making music, it's *dead*, just so much wood and gut!"

Jenny smiled and shook her head.

"Oh, Ma's got a totally anthropomorphic view of things as well as animals," Michael said. "She probably thinks the poor violin feels lonely and frustrated."

"No," I said defensively, "it's just that I hate seeing things that are meant to be used being treated as objects for purely materialistic ends."

I MADE the gingerbread and took it round to Rosemary, who was being a sort of clearinghouse for bonfire night contributions.

"Oh, lovely," she said. "Bonfire night wouldn't be the same without gingerbread. Or is it parkin?"

"I think you're only allowed to call it that in York-

159

shire," I said, "though I believe the recipe's the same. How's it going?"

"I've got that chest freezer out in the utility room *full* of food of various kinds," Rosemary replied. "Just as well the family's here and we've eaten up most of this summer's veg. There wouldn't have been room otherwise. Oh, did I tell you? They're hoping to get completion on the house next week. I'm so glad you told me about the Welches—it's a perfect house for them."

"So when will they move?" I asked.

"In about a fortnight. Roger's hoping to get a few days off to help, but what with this Graham case, I don't know if he will. Talking of which, *what* an extraordinary thing about that trust thing. Does it really mean that Ronnie and Carol will be fabulously rich?"

"Well, I don't know how much you know," I said tentatively, "and I'm probably not supposed to say anything at all really, since I got it from Michael in confidence, but—yes, it does look like that."

"I only hope it improves Carol's temper," Rosemary said. "She and Ronnie were having the most awful row in the shop the other day. I was in there with Jilly, trying to buy some shoes for Delia—oh, it's *so* difficult. The child has taken against shoes for some reason, and she simply sat on the floor and *howled* when poor Jilly tried to fit anything on her; so embarrassing!"

"What was the row about?" I asked curiously. "Could you hear?"

"Well, they were out in the back, in the stockroom, so mostly I could only hear raised voices and a general angry *blur,* but I did hear the word 'development' several times and Carol saying something about not being taken for a fool."

"Goodness!" I exclaimed. "I wonder what *that* can have been about? The development must have something to do with the trust—you know a developer wants to buy the land for some incredible amount— it sounds as if they're quarreling about the money already."

"Oh, well, you know what they say about money not buying happiness," Rosemary said. "But it's not like Ronnie to stand up to Carol in any way. You know how feeble he's always been."

"Well, money does funny things to people, especially a really big amount like this. Perhaps," I suggested, "he wants to blow the lot on some fabulous piece of furniture or a Gainsborough or something!"

"I must say," Rosemary said thoughtfully, "I was very surprised to see what lovely pieces he's collected. Still waters run deep, or whatever it is they say."

"The row must have been pretty serious for Carol to sound off like that, in the shop where anyone could hear," I said. "She's usually very conscious of the customers. What really makes me so sad is to think of poor Miss Graham! If only all this had come a couple of years earlier, what a difference it would have made for her. It's so unfair—with money like that she could have lived *anywhere* and there'd have been no hassle with horrible Dr. Cowley."

"I gather, from what Roger's let slip, that Dr. C's no longer a suspect," Rosemary said.

"No, he appears to have an alibi. Anyway, all this money seems a much better motive. Except that the two people who benefit don't seem to have known anything about it. It really is a complete mystery. Oh, well, I daresay we'll discover sooner or later what it was all about. How's the cake situation now?"

"I think we're okay. Oh, by the way, that Jenny Drummond of yours brought a tin full of the most delicious brownies round yesterday. She is a nice girl. Is Michael still going out with her?"

"We-ell," I said cautiously, "he doesn't seem to be going *out* with her exactly, not in that sense. I mean they play badminton together, they've been to the cinema in Taunton, she's been for supper with us a couple of times, and they're going to the bonfire thing together, but that's all really. I get the feeling that Michael's just someone from work that she gets on well with, nothing else. And, of course, Michael is his usual clamlike self, and if I asked him about it he'd just make his usual remarks about the CIA! I think he likes her as someone to go about with, but nothing serious. Actually, I'm quite glad really. She's a nice girl and very easy to get on with—I like her a lot—but she's very *self-contained,* if you know what I mean. It's not easy to know what she's thinking. And that's not Michael's way at all."

"Oh, children!" Rosemary said. "Thank goodness Jilly's married and settled down—though, of course, that's nothing to go by nowadays, alas! I used to think that when they were grown up it would be easier—big joke!"

"Absolutely," I said. "Did you know that Fanny Burney, in her old age, had to take lodgings near her brilliant but erratic son, just to make sure that he got up in time to carry out his clerical duties! And he was in his thirties!"

"All down the ages, dear!" Rosemary said resignedly. "Right from the cave!"

· 13 ·

They'd already lit the huge bonfire when I got to the recreation ground, and I could hear it crackling and flaring away as I went round the edge of the ground to the pavilion where the food was being assembled. Rosemary and Anthea were laying out sausage rolls on plates.

"I wonder who first had the idea of putting bits of sausage into pastry," Rosemary said thoughtfully. "There really ought to be a commemorative plaque somewhere. What on earth would we do without them?"

"I could quite easily do without Mary Reynold's sausage rolls," Anthea said, holding up a plate with a dozen or so grayish rectangular objects on it. "Whole meal pastry and heavy as a brick!"

"They don't look very appetizing," I agreed. "Still, it's dark outside, and when the young are hungry they don't seem to notice *what* they're eating."

"Harben's turned up trumps," Rosemary said (Harben's one of our local butchers), "pork chops *and* chicken drumsticks as well as sausages for the barbecue!"

"He wants to be the next treasurer of the Round Table," Anthea said sardonically. "He's casting his bread upon the waters."

"As long as he's casting other things as well, I for one am not going to complain!" Rosemary said and laughed.

"I don't suppose Jilly's been able to get along tonight?" I asked Rosemary as I began pricking baking potatoes ready for the microwave.

"No, she's at home with the baby. Roger's here, though, with Delia. *I* think she's far too young, but she wanted to come. They'll only stay for a bit, just for the early session with the sparklers and those pretty fireworks that don't have bangs—golden rain and catherine wheels and things like that."

"They're really the only ones I like," I said. "Even rockets are a bit scary, and looking up at them gives me vertigo! There, there's a couple of dishes of potatoes done. What's in this tin?" I opened a large cake tin. "Goodness! An enormous Dundee cake—it looks fabulous. Whose is it?"

Anthea looked up from sorting out plastic knives and forks into piles.

"Oh, Carol Graham brought that in," she said.

"Really!" I exclaimed. "Did she make it herself, I wonder?"

"Oh, yes, she's a marvelous cook. She made some gorgeous maids of honor for a coffee morning I did last year for the Wildlife Fund."

"Maids of honor?" Rosemary said vaguely.

"Yes, you know, those little almond tartlets. Very delicious. But of course she can't do very much because she's so busy in the shop. Between ourselves, I don't think Ronnie's much use."

Almond tartlets. All sorts of thoughts were whirling round in my head, but I didn't seem able to put them together coherently.

"She's here tonight," Anthea went on, "because Ronnie can't make it—some sort of meeting—and he was supposed to be one of the official people letting off the fireworks. Carol didn't want to let everyone down, so she said she'd do it instead."

Anthea, I remembered, had always been rather a friend of Carol's and, as such, inclined to be disparaging of Ronnie.

"That was good of her," I said. "It's not the sort of job I'd care to do myself."

"Oh, well," Anthea said, "*Carol's* a very *practical* person, very efficient."

Rosemary gave a little snort of imperfectly suppressed laughter. Our friend Anthea is the sort of person who always says things as they occur to her without considering whether or not they might be better phrased in order not to give offense.

"Shall I cut up Carol's cake?" I asked. "She's cleverly baked it in a square tin so it'll be easier to divide up."

"Better leave it for a bit," Rosemary said. "People will want cake *after* all the other things, and if you cut it now it'll get a bit dry, especially in here with this electric heater blasting away."

"That was Jim Symonds," Anthea said with some asperity. "I told him that we only needed it at half strength but he never listens, and by the time I got here the place was like an oven. All those tuna-fish sandwiches are beginning to get quite dry, even though I covered them with a tea cloth."

"I know," Rosemary said. "I had to take my cardy off, it was so hot. Anyway, what about the urn? Whose turn is it to do it?"

I groaned. The urn, a temperamental monster that plays a prominent part in most Taviscombe social functions (being passed from one organization to another like the eye of the Granae), is my particular bête noir. It is as stubborn as a mule and as temperamental as a prima donna. It needs to be filled with immense care to *exactly* the right level (a millimeter more or less, and disaster ensues), and even then it has a nasty habit of spitting out puffs of scalding steam or little jets of boiling water when one least expects it. Its small tap is either too loose (an uncontrollable flood of boiling water) or too tight (a few miserable drops with a long, impatient queue forming behind the unhappy person manipulating it), and on one memorable occasion, the whole thing tipped right over, almost scalding poor Miss Webber and ruining the new parquet flooring just laid down in the Methodist church hall.

"Oh, Lord," I said, "it's me! Well, for the first session anyway. Liz Priory said she'd take over when she comes—she seems quite brave about it, but then, she's lived with that terrible sister of hers for twenty years, so I suppose a recalcitrant urn is child's play after that!"

Actually, Liz arrived quite early and released me to go out and have a look at the fireworks.

"Hello, Ma." Michael and Jenny materialized out of the darkness.

"Hello, are you enjoying it?" I asked Jenny.

"It's *lovely!*" she said, her eyes shining with enthusiasm in the light of the bonfire. "Really super! And lots more fireworks to come!"

"It was so good of you to make those lovely brownies," I said. "They were greatly appreciated."

"Oh, that was nothing," she replied. "I love baking, as you know. Isn't it lucky it's such a nice dry evening—what would have happened if it had rained?"

"Oh, everyone would have stood about getting wet while the fireworks were set off," I said, laughing. "Then we'd all have squashed bad-temperedly into the pavilion to eat up the cold food, and someone would have tried to build a sort of shelter outside for the barbecue, which wouldn't have worked, and the children would have been cross and whiny, and I for one would have gone home!"

"Well, *aren't* we lucky it's dry. Though it is a bit chilly." She rubbed her hands together and thrust them into her pockets. "I think I must have left my gloves in the car."

"I'll go and have a look for them," Michael said.

"No," she protested. "It's miles away right on the other side of the car park!"

"That's okay," he said good-humoredly, "I won't be long."

"Oh, dear," Jenny said, "I didn't mean for him to go traipsing all the way back to the car and miss the fun."

"Oh, it'll go on for ages yet," I said. "All the really big rockets and set pieces and things are still to come. Oh, excuse me for a moment, there's someone I need to speak to. See you later."

I had just intercepted Freda Braithwaite, who was wandering about with piles of extra paper plates and napkins, and had pointed her in the direction of the pavilion, when I saw Roger with Delia perched on his shoulders.

"Hello, Roger," I said. "Nice to see you here. How's Delia enjoying it?"

"Bang!" Delia said imperiously. "More bang bang!"

She grasped Roger's head with both her tiny hands to keep her balance and twisted round on his shoulder to see what was happening on the far side of the field.

"Oh, well," I said, "*she's* not nervous then. Rosemary thought she might be."

"No way!" Roger said, laughing. "The louder the better! So I thought she could stay for a bit longer."

A rocket soared up into the sky, and Delia gave a little crow of laughter. "Whoo!" she cried. "Bang?" she asked hopefully as the bright stars fell to earth.

I left them to contemplate the new batch of fireworks just going off and started to make my way round the field. As I passed a small trestle table where Carol was laying out a splendid lot of rockets, I paused to have a word.

"I do think it's brave of you to set these things off," I said.

"Well, Ronnie made a muddle with the dates and he's got a CPRE meeting tonight, so I said I'd do it instead. I don't mind really. They're quite safe if you treat them carefully." She took another rocket from the box lying on the ground behind her and put it with the others.

"There, that's the lot now. I'm a bit behind because, when I'd just got started with these, I had to go and borrow some of those special tapers to light them with—Ronnie was going to get some from Dawson's, but of course he forgot. Fortunately Dick Mabey had some he could lend me."

There was the usual irritable note in her voice

that I always heard when she was speaking of her husband.

"Well," I said hastily, "it's certainly an impressive array. When do you set them off?"

"In about five minutes, when Dick's finished his lot."

"Oh, good," I replied. "I'll wait around and see them before I go back and relieve Liz on the urn."

I moved a short distance away to chat with Muriel Mabey, who was standing by Dick's table while he was in the roped-off area where the fireworks were actually lit.

"It's a really good turnout this year," Muriel said. "We should clear £800 at least."

"And everyone seems to be enjoying themselves in a reasonably peaceful manner," I said.

"There were a couple of lads letting off firecrackers over the other side," Muriel said, "but Dick and Ken sorted them out."

"Oh, well, I suppose you always get a bit of that sort of thing. Oh, look! Wasn't that one gorgeous!"

Dick, having shot his bolt, as it were, with a particularly spectacular rocket, stepped back over the rope and joined us.

"That was really *super,* Dick," I said.

"Not bad, was it? I think Carol's next. It was very good of her to step in when Ronnie couldn't make it. Mind you, I offered to do their lot as well—it wouldn't have been any trouble—but Carol said she wanted to do it, so . . ."

Carol let off a trio of rockets in swift succession, and the air was full of brightness—gold and red and green, lighting up Carol's face as she, intent on her task, reached back over the table to select another firework. One after the other, the graceful arcs of light shattered into a thousand stars.

"Oh, dear," I said to Muriel. "I really ought to be getting back to help with the food. There's always a rush just after the fireworks are finished. Oh, well, I'll just watch one more."

Carol picked up another rocket from the table, set it on the frame, and applied the taper. There was a tremendous bang and a violent explosion. Suddenly the air was full of acrid smoke, and debris seemed to be scattered in the air—earth, wood, bits of metal. Beside me, Muriel Mabey gave a cry and clutched her shoulder. Everything was in confusion. People were rushing in all directions, children were crying, and a woman was screaming. I was knocked to the ground, and for a moment I was afraid I was going to be trampled as people rushed past me in a panic. But I was so stunned by the noise and confusion that I simply lay there. My arm was hurting where I'd fallen on it. In a vague way I hoped I hadn't broken anything, but it seemed too difficult to move, let alone get to my feet.

"Ma! Are you all right?" Michael was standing over me, Jenny by his side. He hauled me to my feet and I clung to him.

"Yes," I said after a moment. "I'm fine, just a bit

bruised and shaken." I tried to pull myself together. "What happened?" I asked.

"There was a terrific bang," Jenny said. "We were just going over to the pavilion to get something to eat . . ."

She looked upset and confused, and Michael drew us both toward the side of the pavilion away from the worst of the crowd. People were quieter now, huddled in groups, uncertain and frightened. In the light from the pavilion windows I could see that several people were bleeding from head wounds. Somewhere I could hear a woman sobbing, loud and uncontrolled. The smoke still hung in the air.

"What was it?" Jenny asked, "some sort of bomb?"

"I don't know," Michael said. "It's not easy to see with all this smoke and everyone milling around. I suppose it must have been a ghastly accident."

"Fireworks," I said uncertainly. "I've always said they were dangerous."

My voice cracked and I found I was trembling. Jenny put her arm around my shoulder. "Come along," she said. "Let's get out of here. We ought to get you home."

We were starting to move away toward the car park, when Roger suddenly appeared out of the darkness.

"Please, can you take Delia. Look after her for me—I'm needed over there!"

He put the bewildered child carefully into Michael's arms and was gone. Delia, not surprisingly, began to cry.

"Here," I said to Michael, "give her to me. I'll take her to Rosemary."

I took her in my arms, and she clasped her hands tightly around my neck and burrowed her head in my shoulder. For a few moments I stood there rocking her, as much for my own comfort as for hers, until she gradually stopped crying.

"Come along, darling," I said. "Let's go and find Gran."

· 14 ·

After the darkness, the light inside the pavilion seemed very bright and hurt my eyes. A lot of people from outside had crowded in, and it took me a few moments to find Rosemary.

"There she is," I said brightly to Delia. "There's Gran."

"Gran," Delia echoed, holding out her arms to Rosemary, who rushed over to take her.

"What's happened?" she cried. "Has Delia been hurt? Where's Roger?"

"She's all right," I said, "just a bit upset with all the panic out there. Roger had to go and help."

"What on earth's going *on?*" Anthea said as she came up to me. "We heard this awful bang and people shouting. Good heavens! What's happened to you, Sheila? You're covered in mud."

"I got knocked over in the melee," I said, "but I'm all right. There's been a dreadful accident—with a firework, I think, but I'm not sure exactly." I turned to Rosemary. "Is Delia better now? Poor little soul, she couldn't understand what was happening."

Rosemary sat the child down on the edge of the table and gave her a chocolate biscuit. "She'll be all right in a minute. It's way past her bedtime anyway. I'll just let her calm down a bit, and then I'll take her home—you two can manage without me?"

"Goodness, yes," I said. "You carry on. If something dreadful's happened, I don't expect they'll bother with the barbecue or food or anything. People will just go home."

"Actually, you ought to go home yourself, Ma." Michael and Jenny had followed me into the pavilion. "You've had a nasty fall. We'll drive you back now."

"I'm all right," I protested. "Anyway, I've got my own car here. . . ."

"Better go back with Michael," Anthea said, regarding me critically. "You look awful. Liz and I can perfectly well cope with things here."

I thought longingly of a hot bath and bed and said gratefully, "If you're sure . . ."

Outside we could hear the siren of an ambulance, urgent and frightening. "Oh dear," Anthea said, "it sounds as if people are hurt."

As if by some mutual accord we were moving towards the door when Roger came in.

"Is Delia okay?" he asked anxiously. "I'm terribly sorry I had to leave her with you like that . . ."

"See for yourself," I said, smiling, gesturing to where Delia, her mouth ringed with melted chocolate, was embarking with enthusiasm on a sausage roll—something, I was sure, that was normally forbidden to her.

"Thank goodness! It was pretty awful out there—people panicking. Good heavens, Sheila!" He broke off, taking in my disheveled appearance. "What happened to you?"

"I'm all right," I said. "But, Roger, what on earth has happened?"

He looked grave. "A very serious incident, I'm afraid. I thought at first that one of the fireworks must have been faulty in some way, there was a bad explosion, but there was a lot of metal debris as well—we need the explosives people to check it out before we know for sure. Carol Graham has been killed, and about a dozen people, including a couple of children, have been badly injured."

"Oh, no!" Jenny exclaimed.

"Fortunately Dr. Macdonald was here, so he was able to look after them until the ambulance arrived."

"How terrible!" Anthea said. "Poor Carol!"

Rosemary came over with Delia in her arms. "There's Daddy," she said.

"Daddy," Delia said, considering him. "Daddy, have chocklit biccy."

Roger laughed a little unsteadily. "Not a chocolate biscuit, but I wouldn't mind a cup of coffee if there is one. It's going to be a long night. We've got to clear the ground so that the experts can have a look and see exactly what happened as soon as possible. And yet, I need to keep track of as many witnesses as possible. I've got a couple of constables and a sergeant going round and taking names and addresses—tomorrow will be a busy day."

Liz handed him a cup of coffee, and he drank it gratefully.

"I was standing quite near to Carol," I said, "but I'm afraid I didn't see anything—anything unusual, that is. I was talking to Dick and Muriel Mabey, who had the next table to Carol's. Perhaps they noticed something."

Roger got out a notebook and made a note of their names.

"Actually, I think Muriel was injured," I said. "She may have had to go to hospital. Oh, dear," I went on, "poor Carol; fancy such a terrible thing happening now, just when . . ."

"Exactly," Roger said. "Just when."

THE DOGS were restless and uneasy when I got in, unsettled by the noise of the distant fireworks, and even Foss, usually imperturbable, stayed by my side, wailing more urgently than usual.

"Look, you go straight to bed," Michael said. "I'm just going to take Jenny home, and then I'll come back and bring you up a hot drink."

"No," I protested, "it's early yet. You and Jenny go to the pub or something—don't spoil your evening."

"No, honestly," Jenny said. "I think we both feel a bit shattered by what's happened."

"At least let Michael make you a cup of coffee," I urged.

"Well," she hesitated, "that would be nice."

"Good," I said. "I'm going to take the animals up with me; they'll only get under your feet otherwise. And they need a bit of human company at the moment."

Jenny smiled. "I do hope you feel better tomorrow."

As I lay in bed with Foss curled up beside me and both dogs lying heavily on my feet, I allowed my mind to return to the dreadful fact of Carol's death. Was it an accident, or, given the large sum of money that she and Ronnie were about to inherit, wasn't it more likely to be murder? But, if it *was* murder (and *if* someone had been able to doctor one of the rockets to such terrible effect), who on earth could the murderer be? Ronnie was the only person with any sort of motive. He disliked his wife, it is true, and perhaps he might have wanted to keep all the money for himself (but there was a great deal of money, surely enough for both of them to fulfill their wildest dreams), and Ronnie—well he was such a *negative* sort of person, it was quite impossible to think of him even contemplating anything as positive as murder. It was well known that he was frightened of Carol, and he would never have dared to plot anything against her in even a minor way. Besides, I'd never found him very bright, and whoever murdered Carol (if, indeed, she was murdered) must have been capable of a greater organizing ability than I felt Ronnie possessed.

Also, now I came to think of it, if Carol had been murdered, the same person must have killed poor Miss Graham, and if it *was* Ronnie then, where had he got the little cakes? Unless he and Carol had plotted that murder together (and she'd made the cakes) and then *he'd* murdered *her* . . . It was all too confusing. I shifted about restlessly in bed, causing Foss to give a muted bellow of complaint as I disturbed him.

The door opened and Michael came in.

"I thought the traditional hot, milky drink would be more suitable than coffee," he said, putting the mug down carefully.

"Do you think perhaps Carol and Ronnie murdered Miss Graham *together?*" I asked.

Michael looked a little taken aback by this question out of the blue.

"And if it was Ronnie on his own," I went on, "where did he get the almond tartlets?"

"A coffee morning or a bring-and-buy sale?" he suggested. "Honestly, Ma, I don't think you ought to be brooding over all that now. You've had a bad shock, and you really should try to get some rest."

"It keeps going round and round in my mind," I said. "You know how things do."

"Well, don't let it," Michael said. "Here," he continued as he picked up from my bedside table a large and rather heavy (in all senses of the word) *Life of Henry James* that I'd been sent for review, "read your nice book and take your mind off it."

"Perhaps I will," I said. "But not that one. Get my copy of *The Provincial Lady* from the bookcase—top shelf, right-hand side—that's the one. I think I want a little uncomplicated comfort just at the moment."

APART FROM a fairly spectacular bruise on my arm I was perfectly all right the next morning. After I'd got Michael off to work, fed the dogs, and pulled up the duvet around Foss who seemed disinclined to get up, I rang Rosemary.

"How's Delia?" I asked.

"Fine," Rosemary replied cheerfully. "She's decided that the big bang was part of the fireworks display, thank goodness, and keeps on asking when we're going to have some more."

"Poor Roger," I said. "He set out for a jolly evening with his child and ended up with a fatal accident. How is he?"

"He didn't get in until nearly two o'clock, poor lamb, so Jilly said. And he was off again before eight-thirty this morning."

"He didn't say anything, I suppose?" I asked tentatively. "About Carol's death, I mean."

"I don't think so. He's got to see the whatever, the forensic people, this morning, so I imagine he'll know more then."

"Yes, of course," I said. "I suppose he will."

ACTUALLY I didn't have too long to wait to satisfy my curiosity because I ran into Roger the next day in the bank. I'd just been wrestling with the cashpoint machine, which sometimes humiliatingly rejects my card for no apparent reason, when I saw him turning away from the counter.

"Oh, Roger," I said, edging him into the corner by the securities section, where we could speak relatively privately. "Any news?"

"News?" he asked.

"About Carol. *Was* it an accident?"

"It seems unlikely," he said. He hesitated for a moment. "Look, Sheila, you're on my list of witnesses, since you were quite close to Carol when it happened. If you've got time now, can we go somewhere quiet and talk? My car's just round the corner."

I followed him out, and he drove us down to the seafront, where we sat staring out at the gray tumbled sea while the gulls swooped around the car, hoping to be fed.

"So it wasn't an accident then?" I asked.

Roger shook his head. "I'm afraid not. The firework was definitely tampered with, and an extra charge of explosive was put in it. And not just that—small metal nuts and bolts had been packed in as well, which made it really murderous."

"How wicked!" I exclaimed. "I mean, other people could easily have been killed as well as Carol!"

"Two people had to be treated for burns, and ten more people and a couple of children had bad injuries from the flying metal, not to mention those who were knocked down and hurt in the panic," Roger said gravely. "It had the same sort of effect as a small bomb. It was a very bad business indeed. We must be grateful that it wasn't even worse."

"Do the explosives people know how the rocket was tampered with?" I asked.

"More or less, from the bits and pieces they've retrieved," he replied. "It seems that somebody took the black powder out of four or five ordinary rockets and packed it into a light copper tube—you know, the sort that plumbers use—and added some small metal nuts and bolts that would be shot out with tremendous force when the thing went off, to make the whole thing really lethal—then screwed on a cap at either end (you can buy the whole lot at any DIY store) and bored a hole at one end for the fuse. The copper tube would act as a sort of compression chamber so that the force of the relatively small amount of black powder would be greatly magnified. Then it must have been wrapped up in one of the real rocket tubes, the stick was inserted, and there you are, a hideously lethal weapon looking like a harmless firework. The fuse had been shortened so that the effect was more or less instantaneous."

"Good God," I said, "who could have *done* such an utterly vile thing? I mean, the only person who might conceivably have wanted Carol dead is her husband, and Ronnie—well, you've met him. Do *you* think he'd be capable of that sort of murder?"

Roger shrugged. "I agree it seems unlikely, but I'd never bet on who would or wouldn't be capable of any crime if only the circumstances were right. Nobody would believe that *you* could ever kill anyone, now would they, but say Michael's life was being threatened . . ."

"Well, yes, I suppose so. But, even so, I really can't believe Ronnie would have the ingenuity to work out such a complicated way of killing anyone. Anyway," I suddenly remembered, "Ronnie's got a perfectly good alibi. He was at a meeting of the CPRE."

"I agree that a committee meeting of the Council for the Protection of Rural England sounds highly respectable, and, yes, I did know that he was there and other members of the committee have confirmed it."

"Well, there you are."

I watched a solitary windsurfer (surely mad at this time of the year, although he was wearing a wetsuit) lose an unequal struggle with his board and topple into the water. The gulls had given us up as a bad job and were making for an elderly lady with a small black dog who had stopped by the seawall and was delving into a carrier bag for the remains of a sliced loaf.

"Of course," I said, having just thought of something, "Ronnie is the one person who might have tampered with the box of fireworks at home before she left."

"No go, actually," Roger said. "All the boxes of fireworks were brought along by another member of the Round Table (a man called Dick Mabey) and distributed on the night. Furthermore, each box was wrapped in sealed cellophane, so if anyone had been tampering with them, someone would have noticed."

"Well, that does seem to put Ronnie in the clear, as it were. How is he, by the way? I suppose you've seen him?"

"Yes. I saw him right away that evening. He seemed pretty stunned then, of course. Then, yesterday, when we confirmed that it wasn't an accidental death, I called on him again. He was," Roger paused as if searching for the right word, "not really *with* me—very vague and not taking in what I was saying. It's not an unusual reaction in such circumstances, a form of shock really."

"Well, if he *is* innocent, then it must all be pretty devastating for him," I said thoughtfully. "First his aunt and now Carol. Not to mention suddenly coming into all that money—I should think he wouldn't know if he was on his head or his heels!"

"The money, yes . . ." Roger beat a light tattoo with his fingers on the steering wheel. "Now *that's* got to be the key somehow, but I'm damned if I can see how at the moment."

"Well, certainly if Ronnie has got a watertight alibi . . ." I said. Something else occurred to me. "I wonder who *his* heir would be. After all he and Carol didn't have any children. Do you think there's a possible motive there?"

"I'll certainly see what I can find out; there might be something. As you can imagine, I'm clutching at straws a bit now. Did you speak to Carol at the fireworks display?"

"Oh, yes," I said. "We had a little chat just before she let them off."

"And did she seem more or less normal? Not upset or agitated about anything?"

"No," I replied. "Just her usual moan about Ronnie not having done something— Goodness, yes! I've just remembered! The special taper she needed to light the fireworks. Apparently Ronnie had promised to get some for her but he'd forgotten, so she had to go and borrow one from Dick Mabey!"

"Yes?" Roger inquired.

"She'd already started unpacking the fireworks from the box on the ground to put them on her little table, so the box was open . . ."

"And so somebody could have slipped the doc-

tored firework into the box while she was not there!"
Roger exclaimed.

"And in the dark, of course," I went on, "not to
mention all the people milling about. It was pretty
crowded by that time."

"Right," Roger said. "Now, had she unpacked all
the fireworks when you left her?"

"Yes," I said. "Yes, she had. Then I left her to
have a word with Muriel Mabey, who was with Dick
at the next table, and I waited with them until Dick
finished his lot and Carol started hers."

"You didn't see anyone talking to Carol?"

"Sorry, I wasn't watching her all the time because
I was talking to Muriel and had my back to her. I
only turned round to watch when she actually
started to let the fireworks off. Then, after she'd
done most of them, there was this awful bang and
the smoke and the confusion, so I'm afraid I rather
lost track of things then."

"It all seems like a series of dead ends," Roger
said ruefully.

The old lady with the dog tipped the remaining
crumbs from the carrier bag, turned it inside out,
and put it in a litter bin. The gulls, looking for a
new food supply, moved on farther up the beach.

"What sort of person could *do* a thing like that,"
I said, reverting to my earlier thought. "Killing
someone that way, so that innocent bystanders
could have been killed and maimed as well, chil-

dren, too—they must have known that there'd be children there! Delia," I said, looking at Roger.

"I know," he said, his hands clenched white on the steering wheel. "I try not to think of what might have happened. But, by God, I'm going to get whoever's responsible!"

"It's all of a piece," I said, "with poisoning a trusting old lady. I mean, both acts are so *calculating*, so devious. Whoever did those things must be totally devoid of any sort of feeling for other people; utterly selfish and self-absorbed, not to mention ruthless. Honestly, I really can't imagine anyone I actually *know* behaving in such a way, can you?"

"It certainly indicates a cruel, pitiless character," Roger said thoughtfully, "and no one comes immediately to mind in that way—at least, not in the context of the first murder."

"I don't suppose," I suggested, "that the two *aren't* connected. Perhaps someone else wanted Carol out of the way for some totally different reason, nothing to do with Ronnie, Miss Graham, or anything. I mean, now I come to think of it, I don't really know anything about Carol's private life. She may have had all sorts of secrets that one simply knew nothing about."

"It's a possibility," Roger said. "Perhaps," he added with an amused sidelong glance at me, "you'd better get the Taviscombe mafia to work on it right away!"

· 15 ·

"Well," I said, "what do we *really* know about Carol? I mean, she's always been a bit difficult and not very easy to get on with, so somehow I've rather avoided her."

Rosemary got up from her chair to put another log on the fire. "She was a bit older than Ronnie, of course," she said, moving the burning logs with a poker so that a shower of sparks fell into the hearth. "There, that's better. An open fire is the very last thing I shall give up when old age finally creeps up on me—it's an awful bore to clean out every day, but there really is nothing like it!"

"Yes," I said. "I sometimes wish I hadn't got rid of ours, but when Peter died and Michael was away at Oxford, I couldn't face lugging coal and logs about so I got gas ones—not the same, though, however many little flickering artificial flames they have!"

"Carol was certainly very blunt and down to earth," Rosemary said, "but very efficient—you have to give her that. I can't imagine how Ronnie will manage without her in the shop."

"Well, he won't have to, will he? I mean, I don't imagine he'll keep the shop now that he's going to inherit all that money."

"I never thought of that. I wonder what he *will* do?"

"One thing's for sure," I said. "He'll be able to buy all the antiques he wants now. I was amazed at some of the beautiful things he's collected—do you remember when we went round there after Miss Graham's funeral? Money will be no object now."

"He'll miss her, I expect," Rosemary said. "Carol used to boss him around, I know, but she organized his life. He'll be lost without her."

"Perhaps he hated being organized," I replied. "Perhaps he just wanted to *be*."

I stared at the flames licking round the new log that Rosemary had just put on and wondered about Ronnie and his newfound freedom. Maybe it had come too late and he wouldn't know how to deal with it. Sometimes the thing we think we've longed for is not the thing we really want.

"There was an old song my father used to sing when I was a child," I said. " 'Just when you get what you want, you don't want what you wanted at all.' Perhaps that's how Ronnie feels now."

Rosemary laughed. "Well he doesn't have to be

lonely, not with all that money. I expect he'll marry again. He's quite a catch now!"

"Oh, dear, do you think he will? Some little gold digger, years younger than he is?"

"It happens."

We both fell silent, contemplating this scenario. Our musings were interrupted by Jack coming into the room.

"Good heavens! Are you two still having tea?"

Rosemary glanced guiltily at the tea things on the little table in front of the fire. "Jack, you're home! Is it that time already?"

"Goodness, yes," I said, getting to my feet. "I'd no idea it was so late. I must be off!"

"No, no, Sheila, don't go! I'm early actually. I called to see a client, but he was out, so I didn't bother to go back to the office. No, sit down and we'll all have a glass of sherry."

"Good idea," Rosemary said, picking up the tea tray. "You pour then while I get rid of this lot."

"Well, now, Sheila," Jack said, handing me a brimming glass, "and how's the world treating you? Are you all right after that nasty tumble you took?"

"Oh, yes, that's fine. But still very shocked, like everyone, that such a thing could have happened."

"Good God, yes," he said forcefully. "I was at that CPRE meeting when the thing went off. Thought it was a bomb. I said to George Prior, 'That sounds like a bomb! Don't say the bloody IRA have hit Taviscombe!' "

"Of course," I said, "the meeting was at Brunswick Lodge, wasn't it—that's quite near the recreation ground—so you'd have heard it! Had the meeting started when you heard the explosion?"

"Only just," Jack replied with disapproval. "Charlie Benson rang up and said he'd be late—damned car wouldn't start or something—and he was waiting for the AA, so we were all kicking our heels for the best part of half an hour before the meeting started. Downright ridiculous having a chairman who lives at the back of beyond like that!"

"Was Ronnie Graham at the meeting?" I asked.

"Yes, poor chap, he was sitting opposite me. Of course, we'd no idea when that thing went off just what had happened. I mean, I've really not got much time for the fellow—a bit of a wet fish—but to have such a thing happen to your *wife*, well!"

"What did you all do?" I asked casually, "while you were waiting for Charlie Benson?"

"Do? I don't know. People were all over the place. You know what a rabbit warren of a place Brunswick Lodge is! I was having a cup of coffee in the big room where they'd got the refreshments laid out, when I got buttonholed by Joan Meadows about that cycle path scheme. Blasted woman! Seems to think she only has to say a thing over and over enough times, and people'll change their minds!"

"Was Ronnie Graham having coffee, too?"

"Ronnie Graham? *I* don't know. As I told you, I had my hands full with that Meadows woman!"

"What about Joan Meadows?" Rosemary asked, coming back into the room. "Is that my sherry, Jack?"

"She was on again about that cycle path—a lot of damned nonsense! Nobody'll use it—look at the one from Dunster; always empty! No, all it'll do is hold up the traffic for weeks with the roadwork and cost the rate-payers the bloody earth!"

"Oh, bicycles are a menace!" I said. "They go about in *packs* now, all over the road, and glare at you if you try to creep past in the car! A bit different from when we used to cycle to school!"

"And those ridiculous helmets they wear!" Rosemary interrupted. "I know they're supposed to make everything safer, but I'm sure they just encourage people to think they're in the Tour de France or something and so make things more dangerous than ever!"

I wondered if Roger had got the full story of the committee meeting. After all, if nobody could be sure where everyone was for that spare half hour, then Ronnie *might* have slipped out, mingled with the crowd, put the fatal rocket into Carol's box when she was with Dick Mabey, and have been back in time before the meeting started. I didn't quite like to telephone Roger and ask him because it might sound as if I didn't think he'd done his job properly. Still, it was a possibility and, as such, should be looked into.

* * *

I HAD a word with Anthea when we were checking over the contributions for the fancy-work stall for the Help the Aged Christmas Fayre. No matter what the tragedy—flood, fire, murder—the Christmas Fayre must go on . . .

"Anthea," I said, "you knew Carol pretty well. Did she have any family?"

"Family?" Anthea looked up from folding a pink knitted bed jacket. "I don't think so. There was an aged aunt of some kind in Stoke-on-Trent, but she died a couple of years ago; I remember Carol going up for the funeral."

"And that's all?" I asked.

Anthea looked at me curiously. "Why all this sudden interest in Carol?"

"Well," I said cautiously, "I just wondered. I mean, there's all that money—you heard about that?—and I wondered if she might have left something to a relative or anything, or if it'll all go to Ronnie."

Anthea snorted. "It really does seem ridiculous, someone like Ronnie Graham, of all people, having a lot of money! What on earth will he do with it?"

"Buy antiques, I shouldn't wonder. He seems to have a taste for such things."

"Well, it does seem unfair, when you think how hard Carol worked—with no help at all from *him*—and just when she could have had an easier life, this dreadful thing had to happen!"

"Yes," I agreed, moving a tray of pink satin lavender bags to one side of the trestle table to make room for a knitted tea cozy and a heavily belaced and beribboned cushion. "From what I can gather, it seems to be a great deal of money."

Anthea looked thoughtful. "Of course," she said slowly, "there was the daughter."

"What?"

"Carol's daughter."

I looked at her in amazement. "But they didn't have any children," I said.

"No, I know that," Anthea said impatiently. "No, this was Carol's child. She was born before Carol married Ronnie. I mean, she wasn't *married* at the time."

"Good heavens!" I exclaimed, "I never knew that!"

"No, nobody did," Anthea replied, "and I don't suppose Carol would have told me, but she was feeling pretty low, she'd just had a bad go of flu— oh, it must have been two years ago—and we were talking and she just came out with it."

"Carol!" I said. "Of all people!"

"Well, she's dead now, poor soul, so I don't suppose it matters you knowing now."

"Did Ronnie know?" I asked.

"Oh, yes, she told him before they got married. I will say this for him, he never made an issue of it in any way."

"Who was the father, I wonder?"

"She didn't say. I gather it all happened when she was quite a young girl, living in Staffordshire.

Nowadays people wouldn't think anything of it, but then it was a great scandal. I think she had it adopted. Anyway, she had to leave home."

"And it was a girl?"

"Yes. She sounded quite sentimental when she told me—wondering how she'd grown up, what she looked like—not a bit like Carol usually was. I suppose the girl would be in her twenties by now."

"Carol never kept in touch, then?"

"Well, no. She wouldn't, I suppose, if it was adopted."

"How absolutely extraordinary!" I said. "Carol Graham, of all people! Still," I continued, "she might have left the girl something in her will. I mean, Ronnie hasn't any close relations, now Miss Graham's gone, so Carol might have thought her daughter could inherit the shop and whatever else they had—before she knew about the money, of course."

"Well, I don't know anything about that," Anthea said. "It all sounds a bit complicated to me."

"Yes," I agreed meekly. "I suppose it does. So where shall I put these nightdress cases and the tissue-box covers?"

BUT IT DID PROVIDE a whole new line of thinking about Carol's death, I decided as I opened up a tin of sardines for my lunch. Foss, attracted by the smell of sardines, materialized from nowhere and began to weave round my feet as I wrestled with the tin opener (thank goodness they've stopped putting those little keys that always broke off on the tins, so that I'm not tempted to try using them) and tried to sort out my thoughts.

If Carol had had a daughter and still felt strongly enough to talk to Anthea about her, she might very well have left her something in her will. She might even have got in touch with her—it seems to be fashionable for adopted children and their real parents to seek each other out nowadays; television plays seem to be about nothing else! I suppose now that illegitimate births no longer have the stigma they once had, natural curiosity can flourish unchecked by any social or moral prohibitions. So, if Carol *had* been in touch with her daughter, the girl might somehow have heard about the money and have come to see her mother. Mind you, I don't think Carol would have been keen to acknowledge her daughter in Taviscombe, even though the social climate might make it possible in most places. But here, there'd still have been gossip and sideways glances, something that a person like Carol, well-known for her forthright opinions and moral judgments, would have found intolerable. No, if the girl had come at all, no one (except, presumably, Ronnie) would have known.

Foss, impatient at my slowness with the tin, jumped up onto the countertop and butted my hand with his head. I tipped out the sardines onto a dish (fending Foss off with one hand) and divided them between us. Actually, the thought occurred to me in a flash of inspiration: If Carol had been in correspondence with her daughter, the girl *could* have come to Taviscombe (for whatever reason) without Carol even knowing. After all, if she'd had no contact with her, Carol would have no idea what her now grown-up daughter looked like. So, say they'd been in touch and the girl had somehow discovered that Carol was going to leave her something in her will (something very substantial now, though neither would have known that when they first started to write to each other) then she *might* have decided to come down, unknown to her mother, to see how the land lay. *Then,* when Ronnie and Carol suddenly became immensely rich, she might have murdered the mother she had never known for the sake of the money. Though, no, that wasn't any good, because the money was actually Ronnie's, so Carol couldn't leave her any of it . . .

I sighed. It was all too complicated and I wasn't really getting anywhere. Still, I was reluctant to abandon my adopted-daughter theory entirely, so I pushed it to the back of my mind to worry over another day and concentrated on eating my share of the sardines before Foss (now looking up expectantly from an empty dish) commandeered them as well.

· 16 ·

"**O**h, good!" Michael said as he looked up from the letter he was reading. "You remember Chris Portman, don't you? He was up at Oxford when I was, reading history, too, though he was at Corpus. Decent bloke."

"Chris Portman? Oh, yes, I remember. An enormous black beard and an earring; looked like a pirate—only needed a parrot on his shoulder! A nice boy. What about him?"

"Well, you know he's written several books—sort of sci-fi—and made a bit of a name for himself? Anyway, he's been invited to give a library talk here this Saturday. I can't think why I haven't seen any publicity about it."

"Oh, yes, I remember now. There were several posters and a sort of display in the library the last time I was in there. I *thought* the name rang a bell."

"Do you mind if I ask him to stay overnight?"

Michael asked. "We can go out for a meal, if it's a nuisance."

"No," I replied, "it'll be nice seeing him again."

"You will come to the talk, won't you?" Michael looked at the letter again. "He says he doesn't expect there'll be many people there, and he needs all the audience he can get!"

"It's not exactly my cup of tea," I said doubtfully, "but, yes, of course I'll come and lend support."

"Great!" Michael said. "I'll go and phone him now before I go to work."

"He may not be up," I suggested. "Unless he's one of those tremendously disciplined writers who are always at their desks by eight-thirty."

IT TURNED OUT that Michael's friend Chris had shaved off his beard, and the earring was nowhere in evidence. In fact, with neatly brushed hair, a good tweed jacket, cavalry twill trousers, and horn-rimmed glasses, he looked more like a country solicitor than Michael did.

"It's very good of you to put me up for the night," he said, shaking hands politely when Michael brought him back from the station.

"Guess what," Michael said. "The library committee, or whoever arranges the thing, had booked him into the Sandringham!"

The Sandringham is a notoriously uncomfortable hotel with vile food and a surly staff.

"Goodness!" I exclaimed. "Well, we should be

able to make you more comfortable than *that*. But it's so nice to see you again, Chris. And how splendid that you've done so well!"

"I don't know about well," Chris said with a little laugh. "I still can't give up the day job!"

"Chris teaches in a prep school," Michael said.

"Oh, well, at least you get reasonable holidays to write in," I said.

"When I'm not guiding the little brutes through the delights of Dutch art galleries or building their characters by camping halfway up Snowdon in the pouring rain."

"Well," I said, "we're looking forward to your talk very much."

"I expect you and the library staff will be the only people there," Chris said gloomily. "That's how it usually is." He turned to Michael. "I'm relying on you to ask the first question afterward. There's always this ghastly embarrassed silence when they ask for questions from the audience, and they all look down at their feet and no one says a word. It's almost the worst bit of doing these wretched things."

"Oh, dear," I said sympathetically, "it does sound a bit of a strain. I do know how you feel—writing the sort of semi-academic books that I do, I don't get called upon to do the public address bit very often, but when I have to, I do loathe it."

"Everything you say sounds either fatuous or the worst kind of self-advertisement," Chris said ruefully. "I mean, if I could *talk* about things I wouldn't *write* about them! And sometimes I catch myself saying the most god-awful crap! Just out of nervousness. Still, you have to do it nowadays if you want to sell a book, especially in my line. There are these appalling conventions, too, when all the sci-fi writers and fans are herded together for three days and nights in some hotel—in the Midlands usually. You find yourself giving talks or sitting on panels at eleven o'clock at night in rooms so smoke-filled you can't see the audience—which is just as well, because the amber liquid's been flowing pretty well nonstop all day, so that by then they're mostly smashed out of their minds. Come to that, so are you, but *you've* reached the stage when all you want to do is to go and lie down somewhere . . ."

"I can promise you," I said comfortingly, "there won't be anything at all like *that* in Taviscombe library."

IN FACT, there were quite a respectable number of people there when Michael and I made our way into the library (Chris having entered by a side door, as befitted the speaker), some of whom I knew—old faithfuls who turned up at every so-called literary event. There were a fair number of young people as well, not surprisingly, since it was much more their "thing" and in view of the fact that the title of the talk was "Science Fiction: 2002."

We sat in the second row (a precaution, on my part, in case poor Chris was one of those literary speakers who hunch forward and swallow their words), and we had barely been settled for more than a few minutes, when, to my surprise, Anthea came and sat beside me.

"Good heavens!" I said. "What on earth are you doing here?"

Anthea is well known for never reading anything other than the *Daily Telegraph, Good Housekeeping* and, at the dentist's, *Country Life*.

She grimaced and said, "Liz insisted on coming— apparently she's a mad fan of this writer person, and she's come home specially for the weekend to hear him. So she made me drive her in."

Liz was Anthea's daughter, training to be a nurse in Bristol, and even stronger-minded than her mother.

"Oh, well," I said, "he's a friend of Michael's— that's why I'm here, out of politeness—and he's staying with us, so she can meet him if she likes. I'm sure," I said, turning to Michael, "Chris would be delighted to meet a fan, don't you think?"

"Oh, is Liz here?" Michael asked. "Would she like to come and have a drink with us after? Hi, Liz," he went on as she joined us, "come and sit next to me, and I can fill you in on the real Chris Portman!"

As I moved in to make room for Liz, Anthea said, "By the way, you know we were talking about Ronnie Graham the other day? Well, there was something I meant to tell you, but I got sidetracked. A bit odd."

"What was that?" I asked with curiosity.

"Well, I had to go down to Evesham a few weeks ago to see Jean Webster—you remember her? Used to be Father's secretary, such a nice woman. Anyway, she's in a nursing home down there, and Celia and I felt we really ought to go and see her. I've been rather putting it off—you know how difficult it is to get Celia to go anywhere now."

Anthea's sister is notorious for refusing to leave her garden at any time of the year.

"But I said to her, 'You know perfectly well there's *nothing* you can do in that blessed garden of yours in this awful wet weather,' so she finally agreed and off we went."

Anthea settled herself more comfortably in the metal chair and continued. "We'd stopped at that service station on the M5—you know, the second one you come to, with the funny name—and were just having a cup of coffee—I must say, the price they charge for everything in those places is a disgrace! Anyway, there we were having our coffee, and who should I see but Ronnie Graham!"

"That must have been when he went to that conference in Birmingham," I said thoughtfully. "I expect he was on his way there or back from it. So?"

"*So,*" Anthea said, "he was with a woman!"

"Goodness," I exclaimed. "Who was it?"

"That I can't say," Anthea said regretfully. "She had her back to me. It certainly wasn't Carol, though."

"What was she like?" I asked. "Was she old or young?"

"Oh, young, I'm sure. I couldn't see her face, and she was muffled up in a coat, sort of grayish, but she had a great mass of fair hair. Quite definitely young. Anyway, Ronnie was behaving really *furtively*, leaning across the table as if he was afraid of someone hearing what they were talking about."

"How extraordinary. Did he see you?"

"No, he was far too wrapped up in *her*, whoever she was. I did hope to get a good look at her when they got up to leave," Anthea said, "but Celia wanted a spoon for her coffee and didn't know where to get one—honestly, she's getting very vague, I really do worry about her sometimes—so I had to fetch it, and when I got back they'd gone."

"How maddening," I said. "Did you tell Carol?"

Anthea hesitated. "Well, I did think of it, but then I thought it wasn't any of my business, and besides there might have been nothing in it and I'd have looked like some sort of busybody, so in the end I didn't. Poor Carol," she sighed. "I'm glad I didn't now. If there *had* been anything in it, at least she was spared that sort of worry."

"Still," I said, "I wouldn't think there *was* anything in it. I mean, not *Ronnie!* I expect it was just someone he met at the conference who was going back sort of the same way—or something like that."

"I suppose so," Anthea said reluctantly. "As you

say, Ronnie Graham isn't really the sort of person who'd be up to any sort of hanky-panky."

The old-fashioned phrase stayed with me through Chris's talk, and I found it difficult to concentrate on the problems of creating a scientific fantasy world when certain all-too-human fantastic scenarios were jostling about in my mind. Could Ronnie have had an assignation with someone? Could he, indeed, have been enjoying a weekend of illicit passion instead of improving his management techniques at the Birmingham Conference Center? It really did seem highly improbable. But if he had . . . A burst of laughter from the audience, indicating that Chris's talk was going well, brought me back to the matter in hand, and I tried to concentrate on what he was saying so that I could at least make relevant congratulatory remarks at the appropriate time.

It was a good talk, and, after Michael had set the ball rolling with the first question ("Would you like to live in the fantasy world you've created?"), the whole occasion went with a swing.

As we milled around the paperback copies of Chris's books, hopefully laid out for potential purchasers, I drew Anthea to one side and said, "Did Carol ever give you any sort of hint that she was worried about Ronnie—well—*straying*?"

"No." Anthea was quite emphatic. "I don't think such an idea ever crossed her mind. Well, would it?

Anyway, it's all water under the bridge now. Liz! Are you coming back with me or what?"

Michael, Chris, and Liz stayed in Taviscombe for a drink ("And we'll probably get something to eat as well, Ma, so don't bother about getting anything for us"), and I went home alone to brood about this unexpected piece of information I'd been given and to wonder how—if at all—it fitted into the jigsaw that was the mystery of Carol's death.

CHRIS WENT back to his prep school ("I can't tell you how marvelous it is to escape into the grown-up world, even for a weekend!") on Sunday afternoon, and on Monday morning, after I'd remade the bed, I decided to give the spare room what is generally known as a good turnout. Firmly switching on the Hoover (the quickest way of driving an over-inquisitive Foss from the room), I vacuumed and polished and washed down paintwork in a positive frenzy, and, driven on by the resultant glow of virtue, I even embarked on yet another attempt at clearing out the second wardrobe that contains garments I hardly ever wear but can't bring myself to throw away.

Such a job can be immensely time-wasting. Each garment is absolutely swathed in memories and can provoke any amount of vague daydreaming. There was that pale blue pleated dress and jacket, for instance, that I'd bought for the wedding of a distant cousin and never worn again but which, in some mysterious way, I felt might come in handy for some similar occasion (though it never had and that was—goodness!—ten years ago); a gray-and-white mimosa-patterned, polished-cotton summer dress I'd bought the year before Michael was born (and which I probably couldn't get into now, though I'd never put it to the test) and which I kept for general sentimental reasons; a silk blouse Peter had brought me from Italy years ago that was really worn out but kept for the aforementioned reasons; a good camel skirt, *definitely* too tight but not thrown out because the material was so good and I Might Do Something with It (though I knew I never would). And there, in a heavy plastic bag, was my mother's fur coat—gray squirrel—*I* would certainly never wear it, but you can't even give fur coats to Oxfam or anywhere nowadays, and I couldn't just chuck it out.

I sighed. What with memories of one sort or another, there didn't seem to be *anything* I could dispose of. As usual, I'd end up by closing the wardrobe door and leaving everything for another six months or so, until my conscience nagged me into having yet another go. I shuffled the hangers forward to get to the back, and there I found, lurking behind a beige two-piece with white trimming (Jilly's christening, over twenty-five years ago), a gray woollen coat I'd completely forgotten about. I took it out and shook it. It was perfectly wearable, I decided. I remembered now, buying it in London in 1982 when Rosemary and I had gone up for a matinee (*Private Lives*, was it? or *Blithe Spirit*—definitely Coward). I remember I'd seen it in Dickins and Jones, bought it on an impulse, and then had to cart it to the theater with me and stuff it awkwardly under the seat. Definitely wearable, nice and full and comfortable, and really quite stylish; I couldn't think why I'd abandoned it. And it wasn't a boring ordinary gray; it was a sort of greenish gray . . . A grayish—greenish gray—coat and a mass of fair hair. A picture grew in my mind of Ronnie leaning across the narrow table of the service station restaurant and talking to Jenny Drummond.

· 17 ·

    I sat down on the newly made bed and thought. Certainly it would fit. Jenny had been going to visit her aunt near Worcester (she'd told me that on that day in the supermarket when I'd seen her wearing the grayish green coat) just about the time Ronnie was supposed to be in Birmingham. They'd have left separately, of course, and met up at the M5 service station. I don't suppose Anthea would have recognized Jenny because, as far as I know, their paths have never crossed. So Ronnie and Jenny met and went off somewhere (perhaps to some romantic Cotswold village) for a few days . . .

    But even as I worked it out, I couldn't believe that Jenny, so bright, young, and attractive, could ever have had an affair with a dim creature like Ronnie—it just wasn't possible! But the feeling that they *had* secretly met continued to grow on me, and I sought around for other possibilities. Perhaps—

yes—perhaps Jenny was Carol's long-lost daughter? She was about the right age and she came from approximately the same area. Say she'd tracked Carol down and come to Taviscombe on purpose to look for her mother, or maybe she'd found out by accident who her mother was when she was already here . . .

She might not have wanted to confront Carol directly and chose to approach her through Ronnie. Therefore she would have needed to see him without Carol knowing.

I tried to remember what Jenny had told us about her family that evening she'd come to supper. If my theory was correct, she'd have known by then about Carol being her real mother, so was all that stuff about her childhood true and the person she mentioned actually her adoptive mother, or had she made the whole thing up?

I got up and went to look out of the window, hoping to clear my mind, which was by now thoroughly confused. There'd been quite a hard frost in the night, and the plants in the borders were rimmed with white. There were tracks across the whitened lawn where the dogs had been rushing about in their first early-morning excitement, and a crowd of small birds were pushing and shoving to get at the seed I'd put out on the bird table. The table was mounted high up on a wall where Foss couldn't get at it, and, as I watched, a gray squirrel lowered itself carefully down from the top of the wall, spread-eagled for greater purchase against the flat, vertical surface, and neatly landed on the bird table, where it drove the birds away and settled down to eat the seed, stuffing it into the pouches of its cheeks with what seemed to me an expression of triumph. I banged on the window but the squirrel took no notice, and I thought that perhaps, in a way, he deserved to get away with his ill-gotten gains as a reward for his ingenuity.

The line between ingenuity and deviousness is a narrow one, and what one might applaud in the animal kingdom should not necessarily be praised in human beings. Murder, for instance, however cleverly planned, was certainly to be abhorred.

I thought again of Carol's death. Ronnie was the obvious beneficiary—unless Carol had left something to her daughter and her daughter was aware of the fact.

If Jenny *was* Carol's daughter, working in the office of Ronnie and Carol's solicitor, she'd have had access to Carol's will and would also have been very well aware of the enormous amount of money that Ronnie now had in prospect. That would fit. But the money was Ronnie's, and if Jenny was going to kill Carol for her share of it, surely it would be logical to kill Ronnie first, and then Carol, when she'd inherited it . . .

I pulled myself up with a start. I was thinking of Jenny as a murderer. Yet as I pushed the thought away, it kept returning. Jenny was a very self-possessed young woman, ambitious and apparently determined to make her way in the world. Looking back over our conversations, I recognized that she had an eye for the material value of things; she wanted the good things of life. Still, that didn't make her a murderer.

Yet I somehow felt that, for all her apparent warmth and her pleasant manner, there was something ruthless about her. Certainly it was easier to imagine her killing Carol in that particularly cold-blooded way than poor, ineffectual Ronnie, for example. She seemed to be a practical girl and highly intelligent, so that the actual construction of the fatal rocket would have been perfectly well within her capabilities. And she definitely had the opportunity to plant it.

I tried to remember in detail what had happened that night. She would have noticed that Carol had left her fireworks unattended when she went off to talk to Dick Mabey, and that was her chance. While she hadn't actually *asked* Michael to go all the way back to the car for her gloves, she'd made it impossible for him *not* to do so. And I'd made it easier for her by going off, too—though I've no doubt she'd have found a perfectly plausible excuse to get me out of the way. Then she simply added the doctored firework to the pile on the ground and left it to do its deadly work without any thought of the havoc and destruction it could cause to innocent bystanders as well as to her intended victim. *Could* she have been so coldblooded and uncaring?

I heard in my mind the tone of her voice as she had spoken about her mother (or adoptive mother) and her aunt. There had been no warmth there, no real affection. Even her description of going home at lunchtime to look after her invalid mother now lacked the ring of truth. Was it perhaps just a story devised to win sympathy, rather than an actual task cheerfully undertaken in the spirit of love?

What I had to do now was to find out if Carol *had* left Jenny anything in her will. I'd ask Michael when he came home.

"*JENNY!* Oh, come on now, Ma! You really have flipped your lid this time."

Michael stared at me in total astonishment. "What on earth made you come up with a wacky theory like that?"

"I just put two and two together and made a sort of leap."

Michael snorted. "Leap? A running jump! No, really, Ma!"

"Have you seen Carol's will?" I asked.

"No, Edward's dealing with that; nothing to do with me."

"But you could get a look at it?" I asked.

"Well, yes, I *could,* but honestly . . ."

"If I'm wrong, then no one will know; and if I'm right, then we'll have helped to catch a murderer."

"I wish you could hear yourself! Jenny a murderer!" Michael laughed derisively.

"Well, then," I said, "who do you think is more capable of murder, Jenny or Ronnie? There really aren't any other alternatives, are there?"

"Yes, but . . ."

"Just because she's a young and pretty girl. 'Look like the innocent flower but be the serpent under it.' "

Michael groaned. "Not *Macbeth* again. When you start quoting *Macbeth*, you're always trying to justify some weird, outrageous theory!" He got up and picked up my sherry glass. "Do you want another one, or is all this nonsense the result of too much of this particular amber liquid?"

"I know it sounds fantastic at first," I said patiently, "but just think it out. It does all fit."

"Only if you force pieces in that don't really go— like you used to do with my jigsaws when I was little and wouldn't go to bed until they were finished!"

He picked up the bottle of sherry and refilled the glass.

"*Anyway,*" he said, "the money belongs to Ronnie, not Carol. So where's your theory now?"

"But Ronnie's a very weak character," I replied earnestly. "If Carol had left her something in her will, Jenny could easily persuade Ronnie to make it quite a large sum now that he's got all that money. She could say that that's what Carol would have wanted. Or," I thought of something else, "Ronnie's very conventional. She could have blackmailed him, by saying that she'd tell everyone that she was Carol's illegitimate daughter. He'd hate that."

Michael sat quietly for a moment, eating peanuts and stroking Tessa, who had come across and was leaning heavily and lovingly against his knees.

I had a sudden qualm. "Are you fond of her?" I asked. "Jenny, I mean. Have I been plunging about in my usual stupid fashion and upset you?"

Michael smiled affectionately. "You do rather dash into things on an impulse, don't you? No, it's not that. I quite like Jenny, she's good company and fun to go out with, but there's something unsympathetic there. And," he said, giving me a quizzical look, "I don't just mean her not being obsessively fond of animals, which is obviously what put *you* against her! But there's some sort of—oh, I don't know, an aloofness, lack of—I don't know what— her manner's warm and friendly, I grant you, but I think there's a coldness, a sort of calculation underneath. She just *might* be capable of doing something unkind or unfeeling to further her own interests."

He gave Tessa a handful of peanuts (strictly forbidden), and she gazed up at him adoringly.

"Oh, Michael," I exclaimed. "I wish you wouldn't. You *know* peanuts make her sick! Still," I continued, "I'm glad about that—your not being *involved* with her in any way."

Michael laughed. "Involved! You can't make me believe you wouldn't have known if there'd been anything like that going on—you, with your CIA training! Seriously, though. I don't think the business about being Carol's daughter really stands up; it's too full of coincidences. Anyway"—he paused for a moment as a thought struck him—"what about Miss Graham?"

"Miss Graham?"

"She was murdered, too, remember. How would you fit that into your little theory?"

For a moment I was nonplussed. I drank the remains of my sherry and tried to sort things out in my mind.

"Got it," I said. "It means jettisoning the long-lost daughter theory and going back to Ronnie."

Michael raised his eyebrows inquiringly. "Ronnie?"

"Yes. I abandoned the idea of Jenny and Ronnie having an affair because—well, it just didn't seem possible. On an *emotional* level, as it were. *But* say Jenny knew about Miss Graham and the trust. Could she have known?"

Michael thought for a moment. "Well, yes, she could. Come to think of it, she was the one who looked up Miss Graham's lease—she'd have been through the file then. So she'd have known about the trust *and* the possibility of the land purchase—the buyer was just starting to make noises about then. And Jenny is a very bright lady. She could well have put two and two together . . ."

"And realized," I broke in, "that it was possible

that Ronnie might be a very rich man one day when his aunt died! Well!"

We looked at each other. "Ronnie would have been a pushover for a girl like her," I said.

"Wouldn't have stood a chance," Michael agreed, "if she'd set out to get him."

"She joined the Natural History Society," I pointed out, "I never really felt it was her thing, but it gave her a chance to get to work on him when Carol wasn't there. And badminton, too. Didn't you tell me at the beginning there was some talk of a mysterious boyfriend who nobody had seen?"

"That's right. And, come to think of it, on that birdwatching thing she seemed to be avoiding Ronnie. I mean, he spoke to her once, and she made some excuse and moved away—I thought at the time it was because he was such a bore, but I suppose she didn't want anyone to connect them."

"I suppose they met at her flat," I said. "Poor old Ronnie! He must have been quite besotted!"

"Besotted enough for him to have known about the murders?" Michael asked.

"I wonder." I thought for a moment. "She's clever enough to have involved him in some way so that she'd have an extra hold over him. I mean, even Ronnie would have wondered who killed his wife and his aunt, and he'd have been sure to suspect Jenny. If she'd made him an accomplice—in however small a way—then he couldn't ever voice his suspicions."

"That's right. And *he* had to be above suspicion because of being the main beneficiary from Carol's murder, so he had to have a really good, strong alibi."

"Goodness, yes," I said. "Jenny must have been pretty fed up when that committee meeting was held up and people were milling about everywhere. That certainly reduced the credibility of Ronnie's alibi, though I'm still not sure that the police know about that. I mean, I only found out because of what Jack said."

"How about the police then?" Michael said. "What are you going to do about Roger?"

I got up and picked up our empty glasses. "I've got no proof, of course, and I can't really go to Roger with just a lot of unconfirmed theories. No, perhaps I'll just go on poking about, with your help, until I find something really concrete. See if you can have a look at Carol's will, just in case. Meanwhile, be careful what you say to Jenny at work. We don't want her to know that we suspect her."

"Especially," Michael said, "if she isn't the murderer after all."

Tessa began to make ominous coughing noises.

"Oh, there now!" I cried. "She's going to be sick. Oh, dear, too late! Go and get some newspapers and a cloth—there's one under the sink. I *told* you not to give her those peanuts! Honestly, Michael, I don't believe you ever listen to a single word I say."

· 18 ·

I saw Roger the next morning when I was out shopping, but fortunately he was on the other side of the road, so I didn't have to speak to him. I didn't feel the time was ripe to present him with what he might well consider to be a wild and untenable theory. Still, I was rather curious to know how far the police had got with their investigations and what lines they were following up, so I was pleased to run into Jilly in Boots. She was trying to heave a large pack of nappies off the shelf while keeping hold of Delia and trying to rock the pram, in which Alex was loudly expressing his annoyance at whatever it is that makes babies suddenly howl.

"Here, let me." I took the nappies in one hand and Delia's hand in the other, while Jilly leaned forward to make soothing noises at Alex who, as soon as his mother's face appeared leaning over him, ceased crying abruptly and gave her an enchanting gummy smile.

"Baby," Delia said to me confidentially. "Crying," she explained. "Lot of crying." She fixed her clear-eyed gaze upon me. "Deela not cry. Deela *good*."

"Not always," her mother said, "alas."

"Two of them must be quite a handful," I said.

"Well, Mother's marvelous—she helps a lot—and Alex really isn't too bad. At least we usually manage to get a reasonable night's sleep, which is just as well, with poor Roger coming in at all hours."

"A policeman's lot is not a happy one?" I suggested.

"Well, he is rather worried about this case. Poor Miss Graham was bad enough, but now this perfectly horrible thing on bonfire night. All those people injured—the children—Delia . . ."

"I know," I said. "To put people's lives, especially children's, at risk like that—Roger must feel it's important to catch whoever did it really quickly, to put people's minds at rest."

"Yes," Jilly hesitated, "there's been a bit of unpleasantness in the local press, which upset him rather. Well, you know how hard he works, Sheila, and how conscientious he is. He doesn't talk about it much, but I think he's beginning to wonder if there might have been two separate killers. I mean—poison and explosives! So different. It doesn't really seem like the same person, does it?"

"I see what you mean," I said. "Does he have anyone in mind? For either murder?"

"He hasn't said—actually he's so tired when he gets in, he doesn't have time to do more than have a quick meal and zonk out. Then in the mornings I'm busy with these two—honestly, I believe I've had more conversation with the *milkman* than I've had with Roger these last weeks!"

"The lot of a policeman's wife . . . ," I said.

Jilly gave me a rueful smile. "Oh well, I went into it with my eyes open. I knew what the job was like before I married him, so I can't complain."

Delia, who had detached herself from my hold and all this while had been hanging over Alex in the pram in an attitude of sisterly affection, suddenly took the blue woolly rabbit that was lying beside him on the pram cover and flung it onto the ground.

"Oh, dear," Jilly said and sighed, picking up the rabbit. "Sibling rivalry time! I'd better get these two back home before Delia really gets started! Nice to have had a chat. You and Michael must come to supper one evening, when things aren't quite so hectic. You haven't even seen the house properly yet!" She grasped her daughter's hand firmly and expertly hitched the brake off the pram with her foot. "Say good-bye, Delia."

"Bye, bye, bye, bye, bye," Delia chanted, looking back at me over her shoulder as they made their way toward the cash desk.

*　　　*　　　*

So I STILL didn't know who Roger suspected. Perhaps he was baffled, a word much used about the police in newspaper crime reports of my youth. As for the theory that there were two murderers, I dismissed it. Certainly the two methods, poison and explosives, were certainly different, but given a really clever murderer (like Jenny, for instance), that difference was simply another example of the intelligence and indeed adaptability—if one could use the word in such a context—involved in planning and executing the crime.

I SAID as much to Michael when he came in that evening.

"Ah, well, now," Michael said coming into the kitchen, where I was getting supper and leaning against the sink. "There's a snag. Well, two snags actually, depending on which unlikely theory you favor."

"Oh, dear," I said, "that sounds dampening."

"It is, I'm afraid. Item: I looked up Carol's will, and there's no reference to any daughter whatsoever. She left everything she had to Ronnie, and he—I looked up his as well—left everything to her."

"Bother! So what's the other snag?"

"Item: There's no way Jenny could have murdered Miss Graham, because on the morning in question she had clients absolutely nonstop all morning—I looked up her list."

"Perhaps she canceled them?" I suggested.

"Wouldn't have made any difference. If she was going out, she'd have had to pass the beady eye of our Josie, who, as you know, doesn't miss a trick. By various devious means, which I won't go into, I quizzed said Josie, and she's perfectly certain that Jenny didn't go out that morning. So there you are—up the creek without a suspect."

The water in the potato saucepan boiled over onto the stove with a hiss, and I turned the heat down and reached for a cloth to mop up the mess.

"So she couldn't have killed Miss Graham." I moved Michael away from the sink, ran some water over the potatoey cloth, and wrung it out. "But she could still have murdered Carol. Perhaps Roger's right and there were two murderers. Say Jenny killed Carol, and Ronnie killed Miss Graham."

"But he was in bed with a bad go of flu," Michael protested.

"We've only got his word for that," I said.

"And Carol's."

"He may have had flu but still have been able to get up and go over to his aunt's."

"But, Ma, can you see him doing such a thing? I mean, Ronnie!"

"I agree that he's not the likeliest murder suspect, but, if I'm right about Jenny, she was the one who planned it, made the cakes, got the digitalis—Ronnie simply did what she told him."

"I don't know. It all seems a bit . . ."

"Just imagine Ronnie totally under Jenny's spell, and everything falls into place."

"Ye-es, I suppose so."

"It has to be—unless Ronnie did kill Carol as well, in that half hour before the CPRE meeting that hasn't been accounted for. It has to be Ronnie somehow, either with Jenny or on his own. There's simply no one else it could be."

"I suppose you're right, but there's no way you can prove it."

"No way at all," I said regretfully. I took the parsnips over to the sink to drain them. "Supper'll be in about ten minutes, if you want to go and change."

I TURNED the theories and bits of fact over and over in my mind the next day but only succeeded in working myself up into a state of frustration. When I'm upset, I usually find myself a household task I particularly dislike and tackle that, so at least I feel I've achieved *something*. The kitchen floor was looking pretty messy, what with spillage from the stove, dogs' paw marks, crumbs, and general grot, so I got out the bucket and mop, shut the dogs out of the kitchen, and set to work. By the time I'd finally got the whole thing clean (how I *resent* the casual way those brightly smiling women in television advertisements sail through these tasks, when I, with exactly the same brands of products, make such heavy weather of them), I had decided to abandon the whole mystery and let Roger solve it all by himself.

I opened the kitchen door to speed up the drying process, and Foss walked in. With exquisite precision he left a line of muddy paw prints in a neat diagonal across the floor. He then jumped up onto the countertop and, walking round, completed the trail, so that it looked like an eccentric design thought up by some way-out interior decorator.

I took a deep breath, counted to ten, and decided to go out. I'd see if Rosemary felt like coffee and a slice of carrot cake at the Buttery. But it was obviously going to be one of those days. When I put the key in the door of the car, it wouldn't work. I opened the passenger's door and leaned across to try from the inside, but to no avail; the wretched thing was broken. Feeling grateful that there was no one to see me, I hitched up my skirt and, with infinite difficulty, climbed across the central console into the driver's seat, and drove off to see my friendly, neighborhood garage man.

Actually, he is. Friendly, that is. He's a jolly Brummie, who has long since accepted with good-natured tolerance that I never, ever, open the bonnet of my car and have no wish to know what goes on inside there. As long as the machine goes every time I turn the little key, then I'm perfectly satisfied. Any information about revs or mpg or whatever, I regard as unneccessary refinements. I prepared to throw myself on his mercy.

"Oh, Ray," I said ingratiatingly, "*do* you think you

could do something about the door lock on the driver's side? It seems to be broken."

He made his usual reassuring noises and disappeared into the bowels of the workshop, reappearing to say that Terry would soon have it sorted and would I like to wait or go and do some shopping? It was now raining quite hard outside and looked pretty dismal, so I elected to wait. I sat down on one of the two black leatherette seats and opened a copy of *What Car*, which seemed to be the only entertainment available.

I was just depressing myself by checking the secondhand value of my car when I heard Ray talking to another customer.

"It's almost ready for you, Mr. Graham—Barry's just giving it a road test now. He won't be long, if you'd just like to sit down and wait."

Ronnie Graham came over and sat down in the other chair next to mine. He seemed to be taken aback when I lowered my copy of *What Car* and he saw that it was me.

"Oh," he stammered, "Sheila! What a surprise."

"Hello, Ronnie. How are you?"

"Me? Oh, I'm fine. Well, not fine exactly . . ."

He looked really awful. He'd looked ill after Miss Graham died, but he seemed even worse now. His face was an unhealthy putty color, the bones standing out almost skeletally, and his eyes were redrimmed, as if he hadn't been sleeping. Actually he looked only half awake, as if he were moving around in a dream.

"I was so very sorry about Carol," I said. "It was a terrible thing."

"Yes, terrible . . ." His voice trailed away again.

"How are you managing?"

"Managing?" He looked at me vaguely.

"I mean, cooking, looking after yourself generally."

He gave a wan little smile. "Oh, I manage, thank you."

"I don't suppose the police have any idea?" I said tentatively.

He shook his head. "Not as far as I know. They haven't said anything."

"It must have been especially awful for you, coming so soon after Miss Graham's death."

There was a flicker of interest, of awareness in his eyes, but he replied in his usual flat tones. "Yes, it's all been—terrible."

"Of course you weren't there—at the recreation ground, I mean. It was so sudden. We were all so shocked—well, you can imagine. Michael and I," I paused for a fraction of a moment, "and Jenny." Now there was a stiffening, a tenseness. "Jenny Drummond—I think you know her?"

"Jenny Drummond," he spoke the name slowly, as if it was strange to him.

"Yes, I expect you know her from the Natural History Society and the badminton club. She's quite a friend of Michael's."

"Yes, yes, of course, Jenny Drummond." His voice was flat again, though I felt with some effort.

"She was with us, Michael and me, just before it happened."

Again, the tenseness and now a sort of apprehension. He didn't say anything, and I went on. "From what I hear, someone put a rocket that had been tampered with—explosives and things, I believe—in with the others. What a dreadful thing! And what a miracle that more people weren't killed—though quite a few were injured—children, too . . ." I felt that I was playing with a fish on a line. "How could anyone do such a thing!"

"Dreadful." The voice was almost a whisper now, and I had to strain to hear it.

"Still, I expect the police will be on to something soon. I'm sure explosives and things can be traced."

He was silent, fidgeting with his hat, one of those waterproof Barbour caps, which was beaded with raindrops that slowly rolled down off the cap and onto the floor.

"And have the police any more news about poor Miss Graham?" I tried another tack.

He shook his head. "No, I've heard nothing."

"Of course, you had that dreadful go of flu just then," I said. "It was a particularly virulent kind, I believe—poor Dorothy Browning had it over a month ago, and she's *still* not right, even now. Actually, if you don't mind my saying so, Ronnie, you don't look at all well yourself. Have you seen your doctor?"

"Oh, yes." His voice was louder and more as-sured. "Dr Masefield's been very good. He's been to see me quite often."

"Really?"

"He's very good about calling. Actually, he called to see me the morning poor Aunt Mabel died."

I looked at him sharply, wondering if he had given me this piece of information deliberately, but he was looking down at his cap again and I couldn't see his face properly.

"Well," I said, "you must take care of yourself. You've been through a dreadful time. Have you any idea what you'll do?"

"Do?"

"About the shop and everything."

"Oh." He shrugged his shoulders. "I haven't really thought about it. It's all been so . . ."

His voice was muffled and he looked out the win-dow, where a couple of seagulls were swooping down with raucous cries on something they hoped was edible. The gray, rainy day outside and the mel-ancholy cries of the birds depressed me. It all seemed hopeless. No doubt Roger knew about Dr. Masefeld's visit (Ronnie would never have men-tioned it, knowing it could be checked, if it wasn't true), which presumably gave him an alibi for the time of Miss Graham's death. That was obviously why the police had never followed up on Ronnie as a suspect. In my own plunging about, as Michael called it, I'd overlooked that point.

"There you are then, Mrs. Malory." Ray appeared, holding out my car keys. "Terry's fixed it for now, but I think we'd better order a new lock, just to be on the safe side. I'll give you a bell when it's in."

I thanked him profusely and took the keys.

"Good-bye, Ronnie," I said. "Do let me know how things go, won't you? And, of course, if there's anything I can do?"

He got to his feet awkwardly. "Thank you very much, Sheila. That's very kind of you."

As I ALWAYS DO when I want to brood about anything, I drove down to the seafront. I sat in the car, watching the tide slowly coming in and covering the sand and the shingle, the lumps of seaweed, and the general detritus—plastic bottles, old iron spars, bits of fishing net, lumps of concrete smoothed by the waves—removing all traces of manmade objects, as if they'd never been.

So Ronnie had an alibi for the time of Miss Graham's murder, and no doubt Roger had checked on the hiatus at the CPRE meeting—I felt I mustn't underestimate Roger's thoroughness again—and presumably he'd be able to account for his time then, so he couldn't have been at the recreation ground at the time of Carol's death, either. He was in the clear. And yet . . . His manner just now *had* been evasive. It wasn't, I was sure, just his way of coping with an intrusive, pestering female. There had been real fear there—that is always unmistakable—and he had reacted to Jenny's name with more than the sort of embarrassment he might have shown if he had simply been having some sort of affair with her. And Jenny, although she had no actual alibi for Carol's death, certainly had a cast-iron one for the morning Miss Graham died.

My mind twisted and turned, mulling over these things until suddenly a thought presented itself, as thoughts sometimes do, right out of the blue. I examined it carefully and saw that it was more than a thought. It was a possibility.

"There now," I said aloud. "I wonder if . . ."

I turned the key in the ignition and drove slowly home.

· 19 ·

I managed to catch Michael on the wing, as it were, that evening when he came home to change and collect his badminton things.

"Michael, which office does Jenny have at work?"

"Which office? Oh, Ma, have you seen my clean white socks—those toweling ones with the blue tops?"

"Hang on, they're still in the dryer, I think. Yes, here you are. So which office?"

"Oh, yes—it's that tiny little one on the ground floor at the back, near the old kitchen. A real hellhole in summer, poor girl. Why do you want to know?"

"I thought it might be. Well . . ."

The telephone rang, and Michael dashed off to answer it. When I went into the hall a few minutes later, he was putting on his socks and talking into the phone, which was wedged under his chin.

"Okay. I'll bring it along this evening. Bye. Sorry, Ma, I've got to dash. Have you seen that copy of the *Shooting Times* I had yesterday? I promised to take it in tonight for Jonah."

He darted into the sitting room, and I heard various things being turned over rather violently until he emerged with the periodical in his hand, gave me an airy wave, and disappeared into the night. I went into the sitting room, restored various cushions and small objects to their proper places, poured myself a glass of sherry, and began to piece together a sequence of events.

I'd gone to bed by the time Michael got in, and the next morning, which was Saturday, he was rushing around in such a flap, packing his things to go away to stay with his friends in Cornwall for the weekend, that I didn't have a chance to discuss my new theory with him.

"Bye then, Ma. I'll be back on Sunday evening—oh, about eight, I should think, but don't get agitated if I'm later. And, *yes*, I'll phone when I get there. Have a nice, peaceful weekend."

I stood in the doorway and waved.

"Take care! Love to Giles and Barbara! Drive carefully . . ."

The car turned out of the drive and he was gone. I went back into the house, turning over in my mind once again the possibility—now, it seemed to me almost a certainty—that Jenny Drummond had murdered both Miss Graham and Carol. The trouble was, I had no proof.

It was a cold morning, and, although the dogs rushed out into the garden when I opened the back door for them and ran around leaping and barking, Foss took a few steps outside, felt the wind ruffle his fur, and retreated back into the house. He looked up at me reproachfully (Foss always assumes that bad weather is my fault, though he never seems to give me credit for the good days), gave a wail of displeasure, and stalked upstairs, where I could hear him thumping on and off the various beds, trying to decide which one to favor with his presence. I did a little desultory housework, looked at the chaos that was Michael's room, and decided (as I so often do) to tackle it some other day. I was restless and couldn't settle to anything, and, although there were several jobs I'd promised myself I'd do while Michael was away, I found myself putting on my coat and going out.

I parked the car by the seawall and walked along toward the harbor, clutching my scarf about me and keeping my head down because of the blustery wind. There was one other person out on this cold, unfriendly day, leaning on the high wall, watching the boats bobbing up and down in the harbor basin below. As I approached I recognized the girl in the full gray coat billowing out in the wind, which was whipping into tangles her long, red-gold hair. It was Jenny Drummond. For a moment I hesitated, unsure whether I should turn and go back the way I'd come, but then with a sudden resolution I walked toward her.

"Hello, Jenny," I said. "What very bracing weather!"

She hadn't been aware of my approach, and, as I spoke, she turned, looking startled and confused.

"Oh," she exclaimed, "Mrs. Mallory! I'm sorry, I didn't hear you—this wind! Are you exercising your dogs?"

"No—I just felt restless and wanted to get out— you know the feeling."

"Yes, I felt rather the same. After all week cooped up in the office, I needed to get out into the fresh air and clear my head and get a bit of exercise."

On an impulse, I said, "Look, if you've nothing else to do, come back with me and have a coffee. Michael's away for the weekend, so I'll be glad of a bit of company."

She drew her coat around her and said, "That's very kind of you. I'd love to. Anyhow, I think I've probably had enough fresh air for the moment."

On the way back, we talked of general things—the weather, the imminence of Christmas shopping, and other banalities—and all the time I was wondering what, if anything, I was going to say to her about the murders.

I dealt with the dogs' usual exuberant greetings, banished them to their baskets, and led the way into the kitchen.

"Come and talk to me," I said, "while I put the coffee on."

I put the coffee and water into the machine and got two cups and saucers down from the dresser. I have never got used to mugs (although I keep a few for Michael, since that generation seems uneasy with saucers), never finding anywhere to put them down that wouldn't cause a ring or a heat mark on a polished surface. Jenny was idly examining my display of china on the dresser shelves.

"Oh, *you've* got one of those George V coronation mugs, too," she said, "like Miss Graham's."

I stood still, one cup in my hand. Then I put it carefully down on its saucer and said, "Yes, that's right. She did have one." I turned and looked at her. "Fancy you remembering."

Jenny's expression was indefinably wary, and I was aware of a sudden tension. She gave a light laugh.

"They're rather unusual, I suppose. I saw it that day I took some papers round for her—you remember I told you I'd met her. She was so kind, gave me tea and cakes! We had quite a chat—I suppose she was lonely—that's when she showed me the coronation mug; she was very proud of it."

"No," I said flatly.

"What?" Jenny looked at me in amazement.

"No, that's not possible," I said. "Miss Graham hated that mug—it was the only thing that her brother's wife let her have when he died; she was furious. She hid it away in her china cupboard in the kitchen, never got it out, would certainly never have shown it to a stranger."

We were standing staring at each other now. There was a flicker of panic, gone in a moment, to be replaced by a smile.

"What are you saying?" she asked.

"I think," I said slowly, with a feeling that I was burning my bridges, "that you saw it in Miss Graham's cupboard when you put away the second cup and saucer—the other you left on the draining board—after she was dead."

"What do you mean? I wasn't there that day."

"I think you were. Why else would you lie about the mug?"

She shook her head. "Look," she said, "I really don't know what you're getting at. If you're accusing *me* of murdering Miss Graham—and the whole idea's utterly ridiculous—then I must tell you that I was in the office all morning on the day she was killed. Ask Josie. She'll confirm it. She was on reception all day; she'd have seen me go out."

"You didn't go out that way," I said.

She stared at me, her confidence suddenly shaken. "Don't be ridiculous. There is no other way out."

"Actually there is," I said. "You forget that it was my husband who originally took those offices when he set up the practice, so I know the building very well. That little ground-floor room that is now your office used to be the old scullery, and there was a larder leading off it with a door that gave out onto the side alley at the back. When the place was converted into offices, the larder was turned into a sort of stationery cupboard, but the door into the alley is still there. You somehow managed to find a key to fit the lock and were able to come and go without anyone seeing you. On the morning of Miss Graham's death, I imagine you canceled or postponed your appointments and slipped out without anyone knowing. Am I right?"

Her face was blank, but I could tell that she was thinking furiously.

"And why," she said, "should I have wanted to kill an old woman I didn't know?"

"Oh, that's easy. You were looking through Miss Graham's file and came across all that business about the trust and the possible development of the land, and you realized then just how much money Ronnie Graham would inherit when his aunt died. That's when you made up your mind to make him fall in love with you. It would have been very easy for an attractive girl like you to cast a spell over a man like that."

We stood there for a moment in silence, and I wondered if she was going to deny the whole thing.

"Why did you have to kill Carol?" I asked. "Why couldn't you just have gone away with Ronnie when the fuss over the murder had died down? Surely there was enough money for all of you."

She looked at me sharply.

"You haven't a scrap of proof, have you, for all this?"

"No," I said. "It's all speculation."

"Who else knows about your little 'theory'?" she asked.

"Michael does."

"But not the police?"

"Not yet."

"Right, then. Since you've got so far, I'll fill in the gaps. Murderers in books always seem to want to tell someone how clever they've been, and I can see why. People are such fools really; they always believe what you tell them. How did you know about Ronnie and me?" she asked suddenly.

"Someone told me they'd seen you together at a service station on the M5," I said, "when you were both supposed to be somewhere else."

"God! This place!" She gave a little laugh. "Yes, we were together that weekend. I had to make sure that he'd go along with the business about Carol. It was important he should have a watertight alibi for the night when she—she died."

"You made that terrible explosive?" I asked.

"It wasn't difficult—all the components were readily available."

"But all the other people you injured—children . . ."

"No one else was killed." Her voice was cold. "Only Carol. She wouldn't have agreed to a divorce, and I needed to be legally married to him to make sure that I got my share of the money."

"But he knew what you were doing?"

"Oh, yes," she said carelessly, "but he didn't have any real option after the first death. That was a pity. It should have looked like an accident. I'd got hold of the digitalis when I went to see my aunt—she takes it for some sort of lung complaint—and if that fool of a doctor hadn't been away, he'd have signed the death certificate as heart failure without any sort of question. He'd been pestering the old woman about her flat, so he'd be pretty anxious that there'd be no inquiry about her death, since he'd have been a suspect himself."

"The police would still have been suspicious about the death, though," I said. "I was able to tell them about Miss Graham's habit of always using her dishwasher, so the neatly washed-up cup and saucer on the draining board would have given you away."

"You've been very busy about all this, haven't you?" she said sneeringly. "Why? Is it just because you're nosy and interfering, or did you have an ulterior motive?"

"Miss Graham was an old friend," I said. "Of course I wondered about her death, especially since I found her."

"And you haven't told that policeman friend of yours about me?"

"No, not yet, though of course . . ."

"And you won't."

I stood, backed up against the sink as she stood

241

threateningly close. For a moment I wondered if she was going to attack me, but she merely said contemptuously, "Because if the police bring any sort of case against me, I shall say that I plotted the whole thing with that precious son of yours."

"What?"

"People know we've been out a lot together—I've made sure of that; it made a very good cover for my affair with Ronnie." She laughed unpleasantly. "And remember, he had access to that file as well. I'll tell them that after both murders we'd have been able to blackmail Ronnie for the rest of his life, wouldn't we? And Michael and I could be living together somewhere abroad very comfortably on the proceeds— it's a perfectly reasonable scenario."

I looked at her incredulously, but she was quite serious.

"That's ridiculous," I said. "No one would believe you."

"You think not? Don't be too sure; people are always ready to believe the worst of anyone. He couldn't prove it *wasn't* true. It would be his word against mine, and I can be *very* persuasive when I want—you ask Ronnie!"

"It's impossible . . ."

"And even," she went on relentlessly, "if the police didn't believe me, mud still sticks, doesn't it? Especially in a little town like this."

I stood there in silence, not knowing what to say.

"Well," she said, "I won't stay for the coffee. I've

got a lot to do. I must see Ronnie and get some money from him if I'm going away—as I think I must now. The first installment that will be, an earnest of *much* more to come. I can find my own way out. Good-bye, and think very carefully indeed about what I said."

The door slammed, and Tris came out from the dining room, barking, to investigate. I dropped to my knees and hugged him tight, as if by making some sort of contact I could free myself from this terrible numb feeling of incredulity and horror. The coffee machine made a sudden grumbling noise, and I realized with a start that I was still wearing my outdoor coat.

The phone rang and, in a daze, I moved to answer it.

"Ma?" It was Michael. "Just to let you know I've arrived safely, all in one piece."

With a great effort I pulled myself together.

"Oh, good," I said, my voice sounding strained and unnatural. "Not too much traffic, I hope?"

"Ma, are you all right? You sound a bit peculiar."

"No. No, I—I just rushed downstairs in a hurry."

"Oh, right then. See you on Sunday."

"Good-bye, love. Take care."

I put the phone down slowly. Then I poured myself a cup of coffee and sat on one of the kitchen stools. Tris sat at my feet, looking at me anxiously.

"Oh, Tris, what shall I do? I *can't* tell Roger . . . I'm sure she wasn't bluffing . . . she's really vicious . . .

and now I suppose she's desperate and really dangerous."

All day I turned the problem over and over in my mind, but trying to think things through simply made me more confused. My instinctive reaction was to keep quiet, anything to spare Michael from whatever horrible accusation she might make. Let her go away; let life get back to normal. But then I thought of poor Miss Graham and Carol. Should their murderer, evil and amoral, be allowed to go free? That would be intolerable. My head ached, and that night, in despair, I took a sleeping pill and sank gratefully into an oblivion where no questions needed to be answered.

The next morning, though, was no better. My head still ached, and I felt sick and lethargic. Like some sort of automaton I fed the animals and made myself breakfast. Halfway through the day, I suddenly thought of Ronnie Graham. On an impulse I picked up the telephone and dialed his number. The phone rang and rang, as though in an empty house. Perhaps he had gone away with Jenny. I didn't know if that made things better or worse.

I sat in a chair by the window and watched the clouds gather over the hill outside, all shades of black and gray, and then the rain came, driven by the wind in sheets across the ground. I sat on, not moving, not thinking of anything now, just being.

I didn't hear the car and was startled by the light suddenly being switched on and Michael's voice.

"Ma? What on earth are you doing sitting here in the dark? What's the matter? What's happened?"

It was such a relief to hear his voice—to know that I was no longer alone, that someone else could think what should be done—that I found I was crying uncontrollably.

Michael took my hand and sat beside me on the arm of the chair.

"It's all right. Everything's all right. Just tell me what happened."

So I told him.

MICHAEL WAS completely certain of one thing—we must tell Roger exactly what had happened.

"But she'll try to implicate *you*," I said again and again.

"Now honestly, Ma, how could you think that Roger would believe that!"

"But he might—and even if he didn't, she'd try to blacken your name. Professionally it could do you all sorts of harm! And you *know* what people here are like! No, we must think about it."

"All right—don't upset yourself anymore. We'll sleep on it and decide in the morning. Now, what about something to eat? I'm starving and I bet you are, too."

I SLEPT better that night, and without a sleeping pill, and the next morning I reluctantly agreed with Michael that we should go and see Roger.

"I suppose we'd better ring first," I said, "to make sure he'll be there."

I was just going into the hall when the phone rang. It was Roger.

"Sheila? Something very surprising has happened. Ronnie Graham has killed himself."

"What!"

"The neighbors became suspicious—and we found him in his car in the garage, with a hosepipe connected to the exhaust."

"Oh, no!"

"The thing is, he's left a note. Apparently he'd been having an affair with a girl called Jenny Drummond, and together they plotted to kill his aunt and his wife. He's written a very full account of it all."

"Good heavens!"

"I think you know the girl," Roger went on. "She's a friend of Michael's, isn't she?"

"They work together," I said quickly, "and occasionally play badminton."

"Oh, I see. I thought Rosemary said . . ."

"Oh," I said and gave a little laugh. "I did try to do a little matchmaking at one time, but that put Michael off, I think!"

"Well, it seems to me he's had a lucky escape— she sounds a pretty dangerous lady!"

"Have you seen her?" I asked.

"No, she's gone from her flat. Her car's gone, too. Ronnie, in his note, said he'd given her all the money he had, so she could be anywhere by now.

We've got a call out for her, of course. Poor chap. I don't suppose he stood a chance with a girl like that."

"No, I don't suppose he did."

"She'd have gone on blackmailing him for the money for the rest of his life, but it wasn't just that—he said he couldn't live with the thought of what he'd done, what he'd condoned."

"That's terrible," I said.

"Yes, well, I thought you'd like to know how things came out," Roger said.

I WENT into the sitting room and told Michael what Roger had said.

"I feel terribly guilty, though. If I'd said something straightaway, Ronnie might still be alive."

"He'd have done it sooner or later," Michael said. "I don't think he could have lived with himself after all that."

We sat in silence for a while, and then I said, "I didn't tell Roger anything about what Jenny said to me."

"But Ma . . ."

"There's no need for him to know. He's solved the murder now, and that's that."

"But when they catch her, she might . . ."

"But *will* they catch her?" I asked. "It's very easy for a woman to alter her appearance—she could cut that beautiful hair of hers and dye it, put on a pair of spectacles, change the way she dresses. She's had two days' start. She could be anywhere. Abroad, even. I think we may have seen the last of her."

I looked at him hopefully.

"Maybe," Michael said. "But that doesn't change things. You know that, Ma." He smiled at me affectionately. "You *know* you'd always feel uncomfortable if you didn't tell Roger all about what Jenny said. What was that thing Pa was always quoting? About always seeing things more clearly from the high moral ground?"

I got to my feet. "You're right, of course," I said and dialed Roger's number. Foss leapt up onto the telephone table, as he usually does when I'm trying to make a call, and I stroked his head to give me courage.

"Hello, Roger? It's Sheila. Look, it's a bit embarrassing, but there's something I should have told you . . ."

Here's an excerpt of the next
Hazel Holt mystery,

Mrs. Malory: Death of a Dean,

coming from Dutton in December 1996.

It's always a treat to go and stay with David. I've
known him forever, and we share so many memories. He
and his brother, Francis, are the children of my mother's
dearest friend in Taviscombe, and their father was our
family solicitor, so we saw quite a lot of each other when
we were growing up. Well, David and I did, being the
same age. Francis was a good bit older, nearer to my
brother Jeremy in age, but they weren't close. Francis
(who was never called Frank, even by his schoolfellows)
was a difficult boy, remote and somehow unfriendly. We
were all rather surprised when he went into the Church,
since he never seemed to have those qualities of compas-
sion and humanity that one would have thought fairly
basic necessities for such a calling. However, he's done
very well—prospered even, if such a word can be used
for a churchman—and is now the Dean of Culminster.

David went on the stage. I think his parents were a
little disappointed since, in those days, it was not considered a "proper job," but they were loving parents and
they supported him (financially as well) for several years
until he established himself in the theatre. He never
played the great roles, but he was a fine Enobarbus, a

lyrical Orsino, a splendidly devious Claudius and a noble Banquo. But even to those who never saw him in the theatre, the name of David Beaumont became what is known as a household word. He was Inspector Ivor in the television series *Ivor Investigates,* which ran for years and years. That was the trouble, really, because when the series finally ended, poor David, like others before him, was so thoroughly typecast that he found it difficult to know where to go from there. A couple of unsuccessful theatrical ventures and a perfectly dreadful situation comedy and he found that he was no longer—what's the phrase they use?—"bankable." It didn't help, too, that his agent was getting old and no longer really interested ("And you see, dear, you can't change your agent when you're on a *down,* can you?") so that the work simply didn't come. People who still thought of him as a "name" didn't consider him for the small parts he'd have been glad enough to take, and apart from the occasional voice-over for a commercial, he hasn't been offered anything for quite a while now.

Fortunately, in the days of his affluence he'd bought a flat in Highgate and a small cottage in Stratford. Lydia, his ex-wife, took the flat, but David had managed to hang on to the cottage, which is where he lives now. It's a very desirable property, being immediately opposite the Memorial Theatre in the heart of the town, and David loves it with a consuming passion. It's become the one fixed thing in his life, a substitute, I suppose, for work, marriage, and family. It is also a minute source of income, since he takes in lodgers, and there's usually a young man, attached to the RSC in some capacity, in the only spare room. Any guests (and David is very hospitable) have David's room, while he sleeps in some discomfort on a very old sofa bed in the sitting room.

"So when," I asked, "am I going to see your new lodger?"

"Julian? Oh, have I told you? He's almost the *perfect* lodger—one simply never sees him. He's got a couple of small parts this season, as well as walk-ons—one of the

Ambassadors in *Hamlet* (lovely for him that they're doing the full version) and Seyton in the Scottish play, so he's out in the evenings, and during the day they have all these workshops and voice classes and so on—absolutely splendid, never in!"

"Oh, I hope I do catch a glimpse," I said. David's lodgers are always delightful young men with beautiful manners, and sometimes they become quite famous and I'm able to say, "Of course I knew him when . . ." Often they owe part of their success to David, who, as well as being the most kindly and generous of people, has a passionate devotion to the theatre and gives a great deal of his time and energy to helping the young, both by advice and by digging up contacts in the theatre for them that he would never dream of using for himself. Sometimes in the days of their success they remember what they owe him. Sometimes they do not.

"Shall we go and see him?" I asked. "Not perhaps four hours of that particular Hamlet, but I wouldn't mind adding another Macbeth to my collection. I think it's fifteen—no, sixteen, if you count that fantastic Peter O'Toole performance that I adored and you hated."

I did see the elusive Julian, just emerging from the kitchen as we got back. He looked a little anxious.

"I had to pop back here to get some more cotton wool—I've run out." He turned to me. "It's brilliant living just across the road from the theatre like this, I'm frightfully lucky—the others are simply *green* with envy!"

"Forgive me," David said, "this is Sheila, Sheila Malory, the old friend I told you about who's staying for a few days—so please don't hog the bathroom as you usually do!" He smiled at Julian, who smiled back, a dazzling smile that encompassed us both.

"Lovely to see you, Sheila," he said. "I'll catch up with you both later. Must be off to work now, do forgive me." Another smile and he was gone.

"A very personable young man," I said. "Is he any good?"

"I think he has distinct possibilities," he replied. "He

wants to *learn* and that's always a good sign, don't you think? Anyway, you shall judge for yourself. Seyton is *quite* a test of anyone's ability!"

It was, actually, a typical RSC production of *Macbeth*. Lots of swirling smoke and leather armor and those World War Two greatcoats that seem to be an indispensable part of their wardrobe. Oh yes, and that peculiar music they seem so fond of, rather twangy and atonal and played on obscure instruments. Birnham Wood came to Dunsinane by means of back-projection and I've never seen so much gore as when a rather over-parted Macduff held up a dripping Thing, alleged to be the head of Macbeth but fortunately unidentifiable.

"So what did you think?" David asked as we sat by the dying embers of the fire in his tiny sitting room.

"Well, he remembered his lines and didn't trip over the furniture, and Glamis Castle *was* rather overfurnished, I thought—rather as if Lady Macbeth had been to some sort of Gothic Ideal Homes Exhibition! And at least he was *audible*—not like that dreadful Banquo, who might just as well have been a ghost from the beginning for all I heard!"

We sat there until quite late, enjoyably picking the production to pieces. After a bit, Julian came in and we told him how good he'd been, and he told us how Seyton really was quite a *significant* character if you looked at the play as a whole, and we all had a nice cup of tea and Julian told us the latest RSC gossip, and we all had a tiny whiskey, just as a nightcap, and after a while I left them to it and went to bed. It's sad, really, how I can't stay up late as I used to. Perhaps, as a middle-aged widow living in a small West Country town, I don't have a lot to stay up late for, so I've somehow got out of the habit.

The next day David and I had a little wander around the town, which is something I never tire of doing. Stratford has, for me, this amazing ability to absorb all the crowds and still remain (in spite of the souvenir shops and that horrid new Shakespeare Centre that disfigures the Birthplace) the small market town it always was, and the half-timbered Smiths and Pizza Hut are so delightfully absurd that I'm quite sure Shakespeare would have enjoyed them as much as I do.

We strolled down Chapel Lane, past the school and along the river, up to the church. It's very touristy now and you have to pay to look at the monument, but that well-known but somehow mysterious bust and the enigmatic inscription never fail to give me a little thrill of excitement.

"I'm glad all that nonsense about opening the grave came to nothing," I said as we walked down the tree-shadowed path through the churchyard. "Even if they'd found something really thrilling, it would have been wrong. They *would* have been cursed, I feel sure!"

"Oh well, the city fathers would never allow it, in case there was something there that proved that the plays were really written by Marlowe or the Earl of Southampton," David said.

"Of *course* Shakespeare wrote them," I said indignantly. "You only have to *be* in Stratford to know that. There are living references to things in the plays everywhere you go!"

We turned right out of the churchyard and walked until we came to Halls Croft, the house where Dr. Hall, Shakespeare's son-in-law, lived. If a grateful nation ever offered me the gift of a house, this would be the one I'd choose. It's a very handsome building, with pale silvery weathered beams let into the mellow brick and, inside, black beams on white walls, highly polished sloping wooden floors, and a splendid staircase. There is a solidity, a sense of achievement and quiet pride, that is very comforting somehow, a feeling of continuity, that life goes on and will continue to do so, steadily and imperturbably, a tribute to the durability of humankind.

We walked through the house and into the garden. "I don't suppose they'd let me be scattered here?" I said regretfully as we walked across the grass beside the great mulberry tree, leaning almost parallel with the ground and supported by a fork. "Still, Michael's promised to donate a memorial seat for me with a plaque."

"Don't be morbid, dear."

"I'm not. I like to think that something of me would be here after I've gone. Do you think it's warm enough for us to have a little sit-down?"

We sat on one of the benches. I drew in a deep breath. "Oh, isn't it gorgeous here! How lucky you are to live in Stratford! And how lucky I am that I can come and visit you!"

"It may not be for much longer," David said.

For a moment I didn't take in what he'd said, then I looked at him in amazement. "David! What on earth do you mean?"

"Well, I wasn't going to tell you—I didn't want to spoil your visit. But things are getting pretty bad. Financially, that is. I may have to sell the house."

"Oh, no!" I cried. "Surely there's some other way? How about the bank? Can't you get a loan, or a mortgage on the house?"

"I'm afraid it's the bank that's pressing for money," he replied. "I've got a pretty horrendous overdraft. And the house is mortgaged already."

"Oh, David!"

"It all started with that wretched accountant—you remember—who made a balls-up of my tax when I was earning a decent whack in the *Ivor Investigates* days. I never really got straight from that—had to borrow from the bank, and then the work didn't come, and one's got to live ..."

"And you've always been far too generous to other people," I interjected.

"And Eddy got himself into a bit of a mess." Eddy is David's son, grown up now and off heaven knows where with some pop group. I didn't think David had seen him for ages.

"Eddy? What happened? Where is he?"

"He *was* in Paris, singing in a club there, but then he got mixed up with some rather weird people—drugs, I think, though he didn't actually say . . . Anyway, he came back to London."

"And he wanted money, of course," I said.

"He was pretty scared of these people, whoever they were," David said, "so what could I do? He *is* my son—you know you'd have done the same for Michael."

"Yes, I suppose so," I said slowly, "though, thank heavens, Michael is a model citizen and far more likely to get *me* out of a scrape than the other way round!"

David laughed. "You make him sound like the most dreadful prig and really he's a very amusing young man."

"Yes, I know, I'm frightfully lucky—especially since he's chosen to work in Taviscombe and share a home with his highly demanding mother! But it's unfair that you should have Eddy's money problems as well as your own. Nothing from Leo, I suppose?" Leo is David's agent.

"There was some talk of a couple of days' filming on location in the Cotswolds, something about a canal barge—it would have been very handy, but it fell through."

"Could you sell something?" I suggested tentatively.

David has a fantastic number of books on the theatre, covering every inch of wall space in the cottage and piled high in corners. He also has a lot of prints and other theatrical memorabilia. It's a remarkable collection, and people come from all over the country to consult it. It's always known jokingly as "The Bequest" because David says he intends to leave it to some worthy institution.

"No," he replied. "Not if you mean The Bequest. You know how I feel about that."

"But if it's a choice between that and losing the cottage . . ."

"Yes, well, I know." He shrugged. "And even if I did, I don't suppose I'd get all that much for it—you know how it is when you try to sell things."

We sat in silence for a while. The beauty of the day and the surroundings seemed suddenly dimmed.

"I don't suppose Francis would help," I asked. "After all, there is The House." The House is the large house in Taviscombe where the Beaumonts used to live. It's in what's known as a very favorable position on West Hill, overlooking the sea, and must be worth quite a lot of money. Mrs. Beaumont died relatively young and David's father was looked after in his declining years by the boys' old nanny, who was deeply devoted to him. When Mr. Beaumont died and the will was read it was discovered, to everyone's amazement, that the house was left to her for her lifetime, and only at her death would Francis and David inherit. What money there was was left for the upkeep of the house.

Francis, who has a very keen financial sense and is one of the trustees, tried very hard to find some way around it. He offered the old woman another house, but she stubbornly refused to move, saying that if Mr. Beaumont had wanted it and had written it down in his will, it would be wrong to do anything else.

David sighed. "Oh, I know," he said. "It is provoking. Just the other day Francis told me that the trustees had a *fantastic* offer from someone who wanted to turn it into a nursing home."

"Taviscombe can always do with another of those," I said, "considering the average age of the population! And it really is ridiculous to think of her living all alone in that enormous house. Can *nothing* be done about it?"

" 'Fraid not—you know how it is."

"Yes, I suppose if anyone could have broken the trust somehow it would have been Francis! Couldn't *you* speak to her, though? You were always her favorite."

"I did try," he said, "but poor old Nana, once she gets something into her head, then that's that, and she's utterly convinced that by staying there—and she's always going on about how inconvenient it is—she's doing what my father wanted. Practically Holy Writ!"

"Well, he certainly wouldn't have wanted you to lose your home!" I said indignantly. "That's what you get, having an old nurse called Nana, like the St. Bernard in *Peter Pan*!"

"It's a great pity she isn't a St. Bernard," David said morosely. "Then we could have her put down."